The Relic

by

Kathi Daley

This book is a work of fiction. Names, characters, places, and incidents either are products of the author's imagination or are used fictitiously. Any resemblance to actual events or locales or persons, living or dead, is entirely coincidental.

Copyright © 2015 by Katherine Daley

Version 1.0

Books by Kathi Daley

Come for the murder, stay for the romance.

Buy them on Amazon today.

Zoe Donovan Cozy Mystery:

Halloween Hijinks
The Trouble With Turkeys
Christmas Crazy
Cupid's Curse
Big Bunny Bump-off
Beach Blanket Barbie
Maui Madness
Derby Divas
Haunted Hamlet
Turkeys, Tuxes, and Tabbies
Christmas Cozy
Alaskan Alliance
Matrimony Meltdown
Soul Surrender
Heavenly Honeymoon
Hopscotch Homicide – *September 2015*
Ghostly Graveyard – *October 2015*
Santa Sleuth – *December 2015*

Paradise Lake Cozy Mystery:

Pumpkins in Paradise
Snowmen in Paradise
Bikinis in Paradise
Christmas in Paradise
Puppies in Paradise
Halloween in Paradise – *September 2015*

Whales and Tails Cozy Mystery:

Romeow and Juliet
The Mad Catter
Grimm's Furry Tail
Much Ado About Felines – *July 2015*
Legend of Tabby Hollow – *September 2015*
Cat of Christmas Past – *November 2015*

Seacliff High Mystery:

The Secret
The Curse
The Relic
The Conspiracy – *October 2015*

Road to Christmas Romance:

Road to Christmas Past

Chapter 1

She felt his presence long before she opened her eyes. Maybe if she ignored him, he'd go away. In the past few weeks, sleep—or rather the lack of it—had seriously become an issue. After several moments of feigning slumber she reluctantly opened one eye and then the other.

"Who are you?"

He sat silently, staring at her from the antique rocking chair in the corner of the room. The light from the window illuminated the shadowless figure as he waited, unmoving.

Alyson Prescott sat up, clutching the pale silk sheet to her chest. "Let me guess. Someone entered me in the ghost of the month club and you're Mr. November. I really appreciate the visit, but honestly, with all the nocturnal visits and prophetic dreams I've been having lately, I'm really falling behind on my sleep. I even noticed bags under my eyes when I got ready for school this morning. I'm sixteen. Sixteen-year-old girls should not have bags under their eyes. Do you think we could do this another time?"

The figure continued to stare at her, not moving, not making a sound.

"I guess not." Alyson wrapped her terry robe around her body as she hunted under her bed for her slippers. Tucker, her German shepherd puppy, wagged his tail without lifting his head from the rug beside the bed as he watched her fumble around.

"I can see you're not going to take no for an answer, but if I fall asleep in English tomorrow, like I almost have several times in the past month, I'll be haunting *you* tomorrow night."

Alyson found her left slipper and stood up. "Okay, I'm ready. What do you want?"

The figure in the chair looked toward the recently refinished Queen Anne dresser that stood in the corner of the room. The light from the moon outside her window illuminated the contents on top. A silver hairbrush, several tubes of lipstick left discarded from her indecisiveness of the night before, a small bottle of perfume she'd had specially imported from France, a pair of 3-carat diamond stud earrings, and the gold medallion she and the gang had found two months before while looking for the heir to the Cutter fortune.

"Hey? You don't currently reside in the cave out on the bluff, do you?"

The medallion had been found in a cave not far from her house, wrapped around the neck of a centuries' old skeleton.

"No, I think we decided our deceased neighbor was probably a Spanish pirate. From the way you're dressed I'm guessing Native American? Although the outfit does seem to indicate that you've probably been dead for a couple hundred years. The guy in the cave a friend of yours? Is that it? Do you want us to bury him or something?"

The silent apparition stood slowly, then faded through the wall into the hallway. "Here we go again," Alyson mumbled as she made her way across the room and opened her door. The hallway was dark. "Up or down?" she asked Tucker, who had followed her across the room.

Alyson heard a sound from the first-floor landing. "Down it is."

She slowly made her way down the stairs, careful not to trip on the freshly polished surface. Her nocturnal visitor was standing in the center of the completely bare living room. The furniture from the room had been moved the evening before in preparation for the construction crew that was coming in the morning to install new floors.

"Okay, I'm here. Now what?"

The ghostly figure simply stood and waited. Alyson began to creep toward him. As she neared the place where he stood, a loose floorboard creaked beneath her foot. He looked down, toward the board.

"Oh, not to worry. We're getting new floors tomorrow. I hope you didn't wake me from the first decent night's sleep I've had in forever to warn me about a loose floorboard."

The figure simply waited.

"No, of course you didn't. Okay, wait here. I'll be back in a flash."

Alyson hurried into the kitchen, which had been completely remodeled a few months before. Tucker followed her into the room and curled up on the rug in front of the fireplace as she sorted through the drawers for the screwdriver she was sure she had seen a few days before.

"Fat lot of help you are," she grumbled to the dog. "You're supposed to protect me from late-night break-ins."

The dog simply thumped his tail against the hardwood floor as she spoke to him.

When Alyson returned to the living room, screwdriver in hand, her guest was gone.

"What, you couldn't wait for the finale?"

Alyson knelt down and started to pry the board loose. "This had better be good," she mumbled. The board came loose and she lifted it away. "Well I'll be."

Chapter 2

"My grandmother hits harder than you guys," Mackenzie Reynolds shouted at the defensive unit of the Seacliff High Pirates. "Come on, show us what you've got. Let's send these guys to the hospital!"

"Mac!" Alyson scolded from beside her. "'Send these guys to the hospital'? That seems a little brutal even for you. It's only a football game."

"No, it's *the* football game. If we win this one we'll only have one more to go in order to make the state finals. Seacliff High has never been to state before. These guys know how important this game is. I don't know what's up with them. They look like they wore their lead underwear today."

"It's only the first quarter," Alyson reminded her friend. "They'll warm up."

"Maybe," Mac grumbled, taking her seat for the first time since the game had begun. "Where's Devon?"

Mac referred to Devon Stevenson, a senior at Seacliff High and Alyson's kinda boyfriend.

"He went for snacks. He asked you if you wanted anything, but you were too wrapped up in verbally abusing our poor football team to notice."

"Darn, I'm starving."

"Which is why I ordered you a hot dog with extra mustard, extra relish, and no onions."

"But I like onions."

"I know, but I was watching out for Eli. I figured there would probably be lots of congratulatory smooches after the game, hence no onions."

"Good thinking."

Alyson searched the bench for Eli Stevenson, the star receiver of the team and her friend of two months. He was sitting next to Trevor Johnson, one of her two best friends and the team's quarterback. They had been kicking proverbial butt all season, making the team contenders for the state title for the first time ever. Mac was most likely correct in her assertion that they could go all the way if the defense would just get the lead out and knock some heads.

"Come on. Get that guy off the field!" Mac was on her feet again, shouting at a defensive end that had missed a tackle, allowing the other team to score.

Alyson watched her friend yelling and waving her arms about frantically. Most of the town of Cutter's Cove had shown up for the big game and at least half of the spectators in the stands were on their feet, yelling and cheering. Alyson had to admit their fever was contagious. At times she found she could barely contain her own impulse to sling insults at the opposing team.

Alyson looked out over the heads of the crowd toward the ocean in the distance. One of the best things about Seacliff High was that it was located on a cliff overlooking one of the prettiest stretches of coastline around. While Alyson very much enjoyed coming to the football games with Mac, she was most grateful for the calming affect the view provided.

"I'm starting to think I should have brought riot gear." Devon sat down on the bleacher beside Alyson and handed her a box filled with hot dogs and French fries. "The crowd at the snack bar has definitely gotten in touch with their evil side. I thought I'd have to get violent just to keep my place in line. People are pushing and shoving, trying to get their snacks so they can get back to the game. And it's not just the students. I saw Doc Robinson cut in line quite blatantly. When someone complained, he said he needed to be at the game in case of injury."

"He might have a point," Alyson defended him.

"The dad of one of the guys on the team is a doctor. He sits on the bench during almost every game, including this one," Devon answered. "He just cut in so he wouldn't miss anything, plain and simple."

Alyson giggled as she nibbled on a hot fry. "I can't imagine Doc Robinson pushing his way into line. The world has definitely gone mad."

"Tell me about it," Devon agreed. "The people in this town are really intense about their football. I've heard that most of the businesses are closed during the games."

"So, you guys going to the Cannery after the game?" Mac asked, referring to the hottest—and only—nightclub in town. "It should be quite some party if these guys stop playing like their grandfathers and start kicking some ass."

"Wouldn't miss going." Alyson continued to nibble on her fries. "I heard the band is supposed to be really good. They're on tour promoting their new album and agreed to a one-night engagement at the Cannery as a favor to one of the owners, who went to college with the lead singer's brother."

"I've heard a few of their songs on the radio," Devon said. "They're really awesome."

"Well, let's just hope we're celebrating a victory and not mourning a defeat," Mac chimed in. "I wouldn't want to be anywhere near Trevor and Eli if they lose."

"Don't worry, we'll win," Alyson comforted her. "I can feel it in my bones, and I'm rarely wrong."

"I hope so." Mac took one last bite of her hot dog, then got to her feet to cheer the team on.

The Cannery, which was an actual cannery that had been transformed into a nightclub, was totally packed after the game. The Pirates had won thanks to a last-minute field goal and the town was celebrating in grand fashion. Fans of all ages seemed to have turned out for the event.

"I hope we can get a table." Alyson looked around the crowded floor.

"The big tables in the back near the kitchen are usually available." Mac started walking toward the rear. "Besides, I'm starving. We can get some burgers or something."

"How can you be starving after the 'snack' you devoured at the game?" Alyson asked.

Mac shrugged. "Don't know. I guess all the stress burned it off. That game was a total nail-biter. Until the last few seconds it could have gone either way."

Devon sat down at a large table near the counter. "Yeah, it was a good game all right. The best one this year, in my opinion."

Mac sat across from Devon. "I prefer games where we get an early lead and keep a nice cushion. Less stressful."

"I just saw Eli and Trevor walk in." Alyson waved at them.

Mac picked up a menu and started to peruse the choices. "I can't decide between the bacon ranch burger and the super nachos."

"Personally, I like the chicken wings and fries." Devon picked up his own menu. "But the bacon ranch burger does sound good."

"Oh, good, you got a table by the kitchen." Eli kissed Mac, then sat down next to her. "I'm starved."

"Some game, guys," Alyson congratulated as Trevor sat down next to her. "You both were totally awesome."

"Yeah," Mac agreed. "But next time let's not cut it so close. I think it'll be days before my heart stops pounding."

"They were a tough team," Eli acknowledged. "There were a few times I wasn't sure we were going to pull it off."

"Would you care to order?" A pretty blond waitress in a very short skirt and a stomach-baring halter asked.

"Sure. I'll have the bacon ranch burger, fries, and a Coke," Mac started.

"Same here," Devon joined in.

"I'll have the nitro wings and fries with a Coke," Eli spoke up.

"Super nachos, no onions," Trevor added. "And just water for me."

"And for you?" The waitress looked at Alyson.

"I'll have a Diet Coke and a seafood salad with dressing on the side."

The waitress walked away and the gang settled in to listen to the music.

"What's everyone doing tomorrow?" Mac asked when the band took a break.

"I promised my mom I'd help out at the museum," Alyson volunteered. "The opening is getting close and she's starting to spaz out about the amount of work they have left to do. Anyone want to help?"

"As fun as that sounds," Trevor said, "Eli and I promised some of the guys on the team we'd go surfing with them. Kind of a team-bonding thing."

"But it's freezing." Alyson shivered.

"Doesn't matter. We have wet suits."

"How about you, Devon? Up for a little dusting and unpacking?"

"Sorry. I told my dad I'd help him out with a new software program he's working on."

"I guess that just leaves the two of us, Mac. How about it? It'll be fun. Lots of sorting and shelving."

"Sure, why not," Mac agreed. "Sorting and shelving are right up my alley."

"Why don't you just stay over tonight? Then you can drive in with us in the morning. I'm sure Devon won't mind stopping by your place on the way home so you can get your stuff. Will ya, Dev?"

"No problem."

"Sounds like fun. I'll call my mom to see if it's okay."

The conversation stalled as the waitress brought their food. Alyson was grateful for the friends she had met since moving to Cutter's Cove, Oregon, after being forced into the New York State witness protection program the previous summer. It wasn't that long ago that Alyson had thought her life was over, but thanks to these friends, she'd found her new life even more rewarding than her old one.

"Maybe we can do something tomorrow night," Devon suggested after the waitress left. "I should be done helping my dad by midafternoon."

"Tommy Bruster's parents are out of town, so he's having a party," Trevor mentioned.

"Tommy Bruster as in Busted Bruster?" Mac asked.

"One and the same."

"Why do they call him Busted Bruster?" Alyson wondered.

"Because he's always having these huge parties when his parents are out of town, which is pretty frequently, and he's always getting busted by the cops for disturbing the peace and underage drinking," Mac answered. "Thanks, but I'll pass."

"Me too," Alyson agreed. "How about dinner or a movie? I think the new Kevin Carter movie is out."

"I loved him in *Almost Dead*," Mac said. "He looked so cute with his hair all long and disheveled. And that scene at the beach, when he was all sandy and sweaty; now that was a work of art."

"In love much, Mac?" Alyson teased.

"Not in love; just in lust. Not that I'm really in lust with him." She turned toward Eli. "I mean, not that I really would do anything with him. Not that I could do anything. I mean, he's a big star and I'm me," Mac rambled. "But even if I could, I wouldn't. Do anything with him, I mean. I just appreciate him as an actor."

"It's okay," Eli teascd. "There are times I think I definitely wouldn't do anything with his co-star, Katherine Colbert, either."

"So, moving on," Devon interrupted. "Is everyone up for dinner and a movie? Say around six or so? I'll check the movie schedule and give everyone a call tomorrow so we can firm up plans."

Alyson nodded. "Let's try that new restaurant on the wharf. I hear it has excellent seafood."

"Sounds like we have a plan," Trevor said. "I think I'll dig up my little black book to see if I can scare up a date. Hate to be the fifth wheel."

"It's getting late; we should probably go soon," Alyson suggested after the group had polished off their meals.

"How about a dance or two first?" Devon grabbed her hand and led her toward the dance floor. "Sounds like a slow one."

Alyson and Mac didn't get back to her place until after midnight. Her mother was already in bed and the house was dark, so they snagged a plate of brownies off the counter and headed upstairs to her room.

"This is so nice," Alyson said as she and Mac settled on the fuzzy rug in front of the fireplace in her bedroom. "It seems like the two of us hardly ever get a little one-on-one girl time. Not that I don't like hanging out with the guys, but this is really nice."

"Yeah, it is. Plus you saved me from a night of more youthful enthusiasm than anyone should have to endure. When I went home to get my stuff I found out that my sisters were having a sleepover of their own. It seems my mom is sewing the costumes for the Thanksgiving play the elementary school is putting on, and there were six sugared-up eight-year-olds running around in various states of undress. It was total chaos. Parts of Pilgrim and turkey costumes were draped over every available surface, a bowl of popcorn was spilled on the floor, and what I suspect were the wrappers from the rest of my sisters' Halloween candy were abandoned everywhere."

"Your poor brother."

"Don't worry; he's staying the night at Stretch's."

"The scene at your place does sound a little out of control, but it also sounds kind of nice. Real people living life out loud, and maybe being a little messy or creating a little chaos in the process. It's always so quiet here. I miss the noise."

"Did you have noise before? I mean, before you moved here? Was it noisy?" Mac asked.

"Well, not all the time," Alyson admitted. "I never had siblings, but it seemed like there were always people around. Friends and such."

"I'll try to be really noisy while I'm here," Mac volunteered.

Alyson laughed. "That won't be necessary, but maybe you and your noisy family could come here for Thanksgiving. If you don't already have plans, that is. My mom just ordered this huge dining table that can comfortably seat half the town, so space won't be an issue."

"Sounds fun. I'll ask my mom tomorrow. Sometimes we go to my grandparents', but she already told me they're going to my Aunt Sue's this year, so we shouldn't be going anywhere."

"Maybe I'll ask Devon and Eli and their dad too. I'm sure they'd like a mom-cooked meal. That is if they don't have any plans. I'd ask Trevor, but he probably has plans with his family."

"You should ask him," Mac encouraged. "His family is weird. I don't mean weird like strange, more like weird like different. They seem to really care about one another and they all seem to get along okay, but they don't do a lot of stuff as a family. They almost never sit down to a meal together, and Trevor has spent the holidays at our house several times because his parents were off skiing in Aspen or something."

"Okay, I'll ask him. It would be fun to have everyone together."

"Yeah, and with my brother and sisters it should be plenty noisy. Just the way you like it."

"I can't wait."

Alyson got up to close the window, which she'd left cracked open. It was a clear if somewhat cool night, with a dark sky and millions of twinkling stars. She looked out toward the rolling sea, taking a moment to listen as the gentle waves crashed onto the sandy shore. She couldn't imagine living anywhere quite as wonderful as this. Closing the window against the night air, she returned to the fire, where Mac was petting Tucker, who looked quite content to have his head lying in her lap.

"I wish I could have a dog." Mac sighed.

"Your parents won't let you get one?"

"No. Mom doesn't want to deal with the mess and Dad doesn't want to deal with the expense. I guess I do get their objections to a certain degree. Our house is already pretty crowded. It's just that I see how awesome Tucker is and it makes me want a Tucker of my own."

Alyson tossed a couple more logs on the fire. "You can come by to pet my Tucker anytime you want. He loves as much attention as he can get."

Mac smiled as Tucker began to snore. She leaned back against the side of the bed and turned her attention to Alyson. "Guess Tucker is trying to tell us it's time for bed."

Alyson laughed. "Yeah, I guess. I suppose it is getting late."

"You look really tired. You haven't been having funky dreams again, have you?"

"Not dreams, but… I was going to wait to bring this up, but I had a visitor last night."

"Who? Did someone break in?" Mac asked.

"Not exactly."

"Then what exactly?"

"It was a ghost."

"Barkley?" Mac asked. "I thought you said he hadn't been around since we sorted everything out about Caleb and his dad's murder."

"It wasn't Barkley. He looked to be Native American. Long dead. Probably two hundred years or so, based on the clothing he wore."

"Wow; so what'd he want?"

Alyson paused and smiled at her friend. "You know, you're the coolest person on the planet."

"I am?"

"Yeah. I tell you that I had a visit from a ghost last night and instead of suggesting I might want to pay a visit to the psych ward, like most people would, you just ask what he wanted."

"Believe me, a few months ago I'd have thought you were nuts, but after meeting you I've gotten used to the strange and unexplainable. Seriously, have you always been able to see dead people and tell the future from your dreams?"

"No, just since moving here, to this town, to this house."

"Well, you definitely seem to be connected to everything mystical in the area. You've done a lot of good and helped a lot of people, though, so whatever is around the next corner, I'm in. Did the ghost need his spirit freed, like the gypsy girl last month? Or maybe he wants us to find something, like Barkley did?"

"He led me to an old piece of parchment that was buried under the floor in the living room." Alyson got the parchment out of her bedside table. "We had the work crew come this morning to tear up the old floor as part of the remodel. If he hadn't shown me where to look someone else would have found it."

"It looks really old. I think it's made from some kind of animal skin."

"Can you read it?" Alyson asked.

"I think it's some variation of Spanish. I can't make out the whole thing, but I think it's a ship's manifest. It lists the people on board, the cargo they carried, the route they were to take, that sort of thing. Look, it's from the *Santa Inez*." Mac pointed to a seal in the lower corner.

"Can you read the back?" Alyson turned the document over to expose a hastily handwritten message.

"I have no idea what this is. It doesn't look familiar at all. It's probably a native language. We'll show this to the guys tomorrow and start working on it."

Chapter 3

The next morning Alyson felt Tucker's warm breath on her face before she even opened her eyes. "You need to go out?" she asked the German shepherd puppy, who had been quietly waiting for her to wake up with his head on the bed beside her, the way he did most mornings. "I'll get changed; then we'll go for a run."

Alyson got out of bed and quietly pulled on a pair of faded sweatpants and a Seacliff Pirates sweatshirt. She almost tripped over the shoes she had worn to the Cannery the night before as she searched the cluttered floor for her running shoes and bumped into the bedside table, waking Mac in the process.

"Sorry. I tried not to wake you. I'm going to take Tucker out for a short run. I should be back in less than an hour; then we can make some breakfast. Make yourself comfortable while I'm gone. There's shampoo and stuff in the bathroom across the hall if you want to take a shower." Alyson pulled a knitted cap over her ears and headed out the bedroom door with the happy puppy trailing closely on her heels.

It was a clear and sunny morning. Alyson and Tucker ran along the bluff and then down the trail that led to the beach. There was nothing better than running along the shoreline as the waves lapped up on to the sand. Alyson couldn't wait for summer, when the temperatures would allow for long days lounging on the beach with only Tucker and a good book for company.

Alyson's favorite books were mysteries, which probably explained why she was so willing and anxious to dive into any mystery that came her way. Of course a steamy romance on a hot summer day could be quite satisfying as well.

Once Alyson got to the point on the beach where the sand gave way to the rocky cliffs, she turned around and headed back. She'd had a lot of fun sitting and chatting with Mac last night. She'd loved her friends in New York, and there was a part of her that would always miss them, especially Tiffany, but she had a sense that her life in Cutter's Cove was going to work out to be even more fulfilling than the one in New York.

Alyson put her head down and kicked it into overdrive as she ran back up the trail leading from the beach to the bluff on which her house was built. The trip down was a lot easier, but the one up gave her more of a feeling of accomplishment. By the time she reached the top of the trail she was breathing heavily.

She slowed to a walk as she approached the house. It would be nice to take a long hot shower to ease the tension in her muscles. She stopped off in the kitchen and gave Tucker fresh food and water before heading up the stairs.

"I see you took me up on the shower offer," Alyson said to Mac as she pulled off her wool cap and kicked her muddy shoes into the closet. "Isn't that shower gel the best?"

Mac didn't answer. Alyson turned around, noticing for the first time that Mac was staring intently at something. "Are you okay? Whatcha got in your hand?" she asked, noticing the picture for the first time.

Mac held it up for Alyson's perusal.

"Oh." Alyson sat down heavily on the bed next to Mac. Neither girl spoke for what seemed like a long time.

Alyson recognized the photo Mac held. It was one of her and Tiffany. Both of them were dressed in school uniforms and were standing in front of a sign that read "Ms. James School for Girls, New York City, New York."

Alyson knew there was an inscription on the back, *Amanda and Tiffany, BFF.*

"I wasn't snooping." Mac finally broke the silence. "Trevor called with a phone number for a woman who wants to donate to the museum and asked me to take a message. I was looking for a pen when I ran across the picture. I know it's none of my business …" Mac trailed off.

Alyson took the picture from Mac and stared at it silently as she tried to make up her mind about whether to come clean with her new best friend. Finally she looked at Mac and smiled a weak half smile. "I guess you're curious."

"Well, sort of. But if you don't want to talk about it..."

Alyson looked down at the photo and sighed. "No, it's okay. I want to tell you about the picture, but before I do, you have to promise me that you'll never tell anyone what I'm about to tell you. Not ever, under any circumstances. Not Trevor. Not Eli. Not anyone. Promise?"

"Uh, I guess. I mean, yes. Definitely yes! I'll keep your secret. I swear."

Alyson wanted to tell Mac the truth. It would be nice to have someone to talk to about her feelings.

Other than her mother, there was no one on this earth she trusted more. She stared down at the picture and lovingly ran her thumb over the faces staring back at her as she began to speak.

"The girl with me in the picture was my best friend, Tiffany. I lived in New York before I came here, not Minnesota, as I've been telling everyone."

"I'm actually not surprised to hear that," Mac commented.

"Yeah, I guess I don't really have much of a Minnesota vibe," Alyson admitted. "Tiffany and I were friends from the moment we met in playgroup when we were three years old. Our parents traveled in the same social circle, so we went to the same events, attended the same private schools, and summered in the Hamptons in huge beach houses with adjoining lawns. We were inseparable. More like sisters than mere friends."

Mac sat quietly, listening as Alyson struggled to find her own pace with the story she was telling.

"Tiffany was special. Different from the other rich, spoiled kids we knew. Oh, don't get me wrong; she could shop and party like the rest of us, but she had a depth the other girls didn't. She had a freedom and spontaneity about her. An adventurous side that often landed us both in trouble. She seemed equally comfortable in high-society social events as playing a pickup game of stickball with the kids from the 'wrong side of town.'" Alyson smiled sadly at the picture in her hand. "She was special and I loved her, and now she's dead."

"Oh my God. I'm so sorry." Mac placed her hand on Alyson's leg. "I should never have asked you to talk about this. I didn't know."

"No, it's okay. I want to talk about it." Alyson looked Mac directly in the eye. "I need to talk about this."

"Okay, but only if you want to."

"This picture was taken just two weeks before she died," Alyson continued. "It was a Friday in April. The sun was shining brightly and spring was definitely in the air. Our goofy friend Alexis was running around taking pictures for the school yearbook, and we were happy to honor her with a cameo provided she made a copy of the photo for each of us. Tiff and I were A-list girls at Ms. James High School and everyone wanted the opportunity to snap our photo. It was such a good day."

Alyson trailed off, sitting quietly for a moment as she stared at the photo. She wiped a tear from her cheek and continued.

"Two weeks later, also a Friday and also a beautiful, sunny spring day, Tiff decided it was way too nice a day to be stuck in school, and that we owed it to ourselves and to A-list girls everywhere to set an example and cut classes. She wanted to see a friend she'd met at some club the weekend before who she was sure would take us wherever we wanted to go."

Alyson took a deep breath. "I wasn't sure about her plan, but before I knew it, she was calling the guy she was talking about. He picked us up in this dilapidated old car, which didn't make me too happy. What made me even less happy was that she asked him if he had a friend he could bring along to even things out. The last thing I wanted to do was spend the day with some random guy I didn't even know."

"So what did you do?" Mac asked.

"Nothing. I should have demanded that this friend of hers take me home, or I should have gotten out of the car and called a cab, but I didn't. I just sat there, quietly steaming, as Tiff's friend drove us through a really bad neighborhood."

"Sounds like a total drag."

"It was, and it got worse," Alyson said. "This guy who picked us up was a total jerk who decided to cop a feel by running his hand up Tiff's leg. She slapped his hand away and told him to behave himself, but that only seemed to make him more handsy. Before I knew what was happening, Tiffany had slapped the guy and demanded that he pull over and drop us off. I tried to tell her that maybe we weren't in the best area to get dropped off, but she was mad and wouldn't listen to anything I said."

"What did you do?" Mac asked.

"Tiff called her dad's driver to arrange to have him come pick us up. It made sense for us to stay put until he arrived even though we didn't like where we were, so we sat down near a brick wall in front of an abandoned warehouse close to where we'd been dropped. There weren't a lot of people around in the middle of the day, and a lot of the buildings on the street seemed to be empty. We'd only been waiting a few minutes when we heard people arguing in a vacant lot on the other side of the wall where we were sitting. They must have come out of the building next door while we were waiting. Tiff couldn't resist the temptation to check them out, so she quietly stood up and looked over the wall. There were three guys: two with guns and one who was tied up and kneeling on the ground. The two guys with guns seemed to be arguing about what to do with the guy who was tied up. I whispered to Tiff that we needed to get out of there before they saw us, but she just stood there. I'm not sure if she was too scared to move, or if she was so totally transfixed by the scene unfolding in front of her that she didn't care that we were in danger just being there."

Alyson took a deep breath before continuing.

"I was about to grab Tiffany's hand to drag her away when one of the guys shot the man on the ground in the head three times. Tiffany screamed and the two gunmen looked up, noticing for the first time that they had an audience. I stood up and got a look at them, then grabbed Tiffany's hand and took off running. Of course they were right behind us. Somehow we got separated while we were running away. Tiffany never was much of an athlete and I jogged every day, so I guess I was just faster and lost her as we ran. I didn't mean to. I never even realized she wasn't right behind me until I finally stopped and looked back."

Alyson was oblivious to the tears that had started to run down her cheeks. "I should have waited for her. I should have made sure she was with me. I don't know when exactly, but somewhere along the way they grabbed Tiff. Two days later the police found her body in a Dumpster not two blocks from where the shooting occurred."

"Oh my God. I am so sorry. It must have been awful. But Aly, you couldn't have done anything different. If you had slowed down to wait for your friend they would have found two bodies in the Dumpster."

"I know that. Intellectually I know that. But emotionally I feel like I could have done something differently. Something better. If I had only made better decisions Tiffany would be alive today. I should have insisted we go to class, or that we look for a cab instead of waiting for her dad's driver, or made her leave as soon as we heard the men arguing. I had so many chances to do things differently, to make better choices, but I didn't. I can't help thinking it's my fault she's dead."

Mac opened her mouth to argue, but Alyson held up her hand. "Don't bother. Everyone has tried to convince me that what happened wasn't my fault. The police, my mom, my court-appointed shrink, even Donovan."

"Donovan?"

"I'll get to him in a minute," Alyson assured Mac. "Anyway, suffice it to say that the whole self-blame thing is really something I'm going to have to work through myself."

"What did you do once you found out Tiffany was no longer behind you?" Mac asked.

"First I hid, then I called the cops. They showed up a few minutes later and took me to the station. At that point I thought Tiffany was still alive, so I did everything I could to stay focused on helping the police find her. I told them exactly what had happened and what I had seen. I described the two gunmen as best I could to the police sketch artist; I only saw them for a second, and I never saw the victim's face at all, but I did the best I could. I cried, I prayed, I looked at mug shots until I thought I would go blind. In the end, though, it was to no avail. Tiffany was dead. The police think the gunmen may have beaten Tiffany in order to find out who I was.

We'll never really know if she told them or not, but in the end it didn't matter. They found out anyway."

"How?"

"After looking at maybe a million mug shots I finally found the guys I was looking for: Mario and Clay Bonatello. They're part of a known Mafia family; the police had been monitoring their activities for years. They asked me to formally testify as to what I had seen so they could get a warrant for their arrest. My parents and I were assured that it would all be very anonymous and that no one would ever find out who I was. Of course the Bonatello brothers have connections everywhere, even inside the New York City Police Department, it seems. The file was leaked, complete with my name, address, photo, birthdate, and social security number. I was immediately put into protective custody."

"So you came here?"

"Eventually. At first they just sent my parents and me to a safe house while they figured out what to do. The Bonatello brothers went underground once they found out they'd been identified, so the police couldn't simply arrest them. The detective we were working with didn't think it was safe for us to stay in New York because it was obvious there was a leak in the department, so it was decided that we'd be relocated via the witness protection program. It took several more weeks for them to erase my old life and create a new one. All in all, we were juggled around between several safe houses for about three months before we were relocated here."

"What about your dad? What happened to him?"

"My dad elected not to come with us when we relocated. He said he wasn't willing to give up his old life and everything he'd worked for, and that he'd rather take his chances staying behind."

"Oh my God. How awful for you and your mom."

"As part of the erase-the-old-life phase, the police killed Amanda and Estelle Parker in an automobile accident. They had a funeral and everything. We're buried in adjoining plots. Once Amanda and Estelle were put to rest, Alyson and Sarah Prescott were born. We were assigned a handler named Donovan. He built us new identities. New names, birth certificates, school records. Everything. Because of the reach of the Mafia, it was decided that he would be the only one who knew where we had gone or who we had become. He's our only link to our old lives."

"Not even your dad knows?"

"No. That was part of the deal when he decided to stay."

"Oh, wow. I know I've said that a lot, but oh, wow. It must have been so hard. On all of you."

"Yeah, I guess. I don't feel too bad for my dad. It was his choice, but I do feel bad for my mom. She gave up so much to be here with me."

"So your real name is Amanda."

"It was. But I really don't feel like that person anymore. My life here is so different. Amanda was all about the newest designer clothes, the hottest parties, and the trendiest vacations. I lived in a penthouse apartment on the Upper East Side during the school year and a mansion in the Hamptons during the summer. I've been everywhere and done everything. I've dined with royalty and been on safari in Africa. Yet somehow, when I'm here in this wonderfully quaint small town, living in this ramshackle old house, and going to a public high school full of terrific new friends, I don't feel like Amanda. I really can't imagine her here. She'd never fit in."

"But don't you miss it? The money; the travel to exotic places? You must have friends you've left behind who you miss."

"Not really. When you're the most popular girl in town, everyone wants to be you, and people stand in line to hang out with you, but no one really wants to be your friend. Not the way Tiffany and I were friends, or you and I are now. I'm sort of surprised to say this, but although I totally want the cops to nail the Bonatello brothers and throw away the key forever, I wouldn't be all that anxious to resurrect Amanda. I sort of like Alyson."

"This is a lot to take in. I'm sure I'll have tons more questions, but I'm not sure my brain can handle even one more piece of surprising news."

"We should get going to the museum anyway. I told my mom I'd be there as early as possible. You can't let on that you know our secret. Not yet, anyway. I need a chance to break the news to her when the time is better."

"My lips are sealed."

Chapter 4

The museum was filled with enthusiastic volunteers sorting through boxes and dusting shelves when Alyson and Mac arrived. Alyson had to admit that between her friend and the founder of the museum, Caleb Wellington, and her mom, they'd designed a museum that was going to be truly awesome.

"Oh, good; you're here." Alyson's mom kissed her on the cheek. "We had another delivery this morning, from one of the descendants of the Chinook tribe that originally inhabited this area. I'm really excited to get everything unpacked and catalogued. We already had quite a few spectacular items from the European families who built the town, but virtually nothing from the native people who settled here before them."

Alyson's mom walked over to the corner of one of the rooms. "Perhaps you girls could carefully unpack and catalogue the items in these boxes. Remember, everything is really old, so handle it with care. If you don't know what an item is, simply number and describe it."

"Sure, we'd be glad to." Alyson knelt down in front of the first box and opened the lid. It was full of old pottery and woven baskets. "Mac, grab that pad and pen and some of those stickers and we'll get started."

The boxes were full of perfectly preserved Indian pottery, jewelry, and household artifacts. Mixed in with the obviously ancient Indian objects were several pieces that looked more European in nature.

"Where do you think this stuff came from?" Mac asked, holding up a silver hand mirror, a matching brush, and an antique music box.

"I'm not sure. Maybe the indigenous people traded with the European settlers. Makes sense that they did." Alyson continued to search through the box. "There may even have been interracial marriages, friendships, partnerships, that sort of thing."

"Yeah, I guess. Hey, look at this." Mac held up an old leather-bound book. She opened it carefully. "Handwritten. I wonder if it's a journal of some type. The text obviously isn't English. I wonder what language it is."

"Let me see." Alyson held out her hand. She turned several pages, frowning as she tried to read. "Although the text is unrecognizable as a whole, there are several words that appear to be English. See, here's the word *boat*." Alyson held up the book so Mac, who was sitting across from her, could see it. "And here's the French word *lisla messe*, which translates to the ceremony of the Mass. And there are a lot of words that are similar to French and English yet somewhat different. Like the word *la pote*, which seems really close to the French word *la porte*, meaning door. Or the word *mus-ket,* which is a lot like our own word for gun."

"Maybe the journal was written by someone who had a knowledge of both English and French," Mac speculated.

"Yeah, but there are a lot of words that are neither of those languages. In fact, the majority of the words seem unfamiliar. Like *mem-a-loost* and *mam-ook*. These words sound more Native American," Alyson pointed out.

"You know," Mac drawled, "the words in this diary seem similar to the ones on your parchment. Familiar, yet not. Do you think this might be some type of hybrid language? A language that was developed by combining the various European languages of the settlers with the Native American languages that predated settlement?"

"It might be. Maybe if we can figure out how to read this journal we can learn how to read the parchment. Of course I don't remember seeing any Native American dictionaries in the library, so I have no idea where to start."

"How about the person who donated this stuff?" Mac suggested. "Granted, being in possession of a book doesn't guarantee you can read it, but it seems as good a place as any to start."

"I'll ask my mom if she has the name and phone number of the person who donated it. Maybe she'll even let us borrow the book if we promise to be careful with it."

Alyson's mom was happy to provide the girls with the information they needed after they explained what they wanted it for, but only after they promised they would stay and help out at the museum as promised. It was late afternoon before Sarah Prescott finally deemed their servitude to be complete, so the follow-up on the leather-bound journal would have to wait until another day.

"There are a lot of books on local history in the school library," Mac commented as the girls were getting ready for their date that evening. "I heard the old librarian was a bit of a history buff, and he managed to collect a lot of local literature that might not be available from other sources. We could meet before school on Monday to see if there are any references to local native languages. I'm pretty sure there are a lot of old documents that provide firsthand accounts not only of local history but legends, folklore, artwork, that sort of thing."

"Sure, why not?" Alyson answered as she sorted through her makeup drawer for a lipstick. "You should try this." She handed a tube of lip gloss to Mac. "It'd be perfect with your coloring. If you like it you can keep it. I'm afraid with my coloring it's a definite fashion *don't*. I let some salesgirl, who obviously didn't know much about skin tone, talk me into it the last time I went shopping."

"What do you think?" Mac smeared on some of the glossy color and turned to look at Alyson.

"It's perfect on you. It really brings out your eyes. You should definitely wear it tonight. And hey, I have the perfect sweater to go with it." Alyson walked over to her closet and started rummaging around. "Here, try this on." She handed the soft cashmere sweater to her friend.

Mac hugged the sweater to her chest. "It's beautiful, but I couldn't possibly borrow it. I'd be paranoid all night that I'd spill something on it."

"Don't worry about it," Alyson encouraged. "It's an old sweater, and besides, I have tons. If you like it you can keep it."

"No, I couldn't," Mac argued. "It must have cost a fortune."

"Not really. Besides, I never wear it."

Mac slipped off her old cable-knit sweater and put the soft cashmere over her head. The sweater fit her like a glove and totally complemented her figure and coloring.

"Wow, it looks great," Alyson praised. "You have to keep it."

Mac rubbed her hands up and down her arms. "Okay, if you're sure you don't want it. But don't ever tell me how much it costs. I'd probably totally freak out and never wear it again for fear of ruining it."

"Done. And I really have no idea how much it cost anyway. I told you, it was totally old. I bought it at least a year ago. Maybe two.

"The guys should be here any minute," Alyson added as she looked at her bedside clock. "You'd better borrow a coat." She tossed Mac a soft leather jacket that had been thrown haphazardly across the foot of her bed. "It's supposed to be really cold tonight. I just got this great new coat I've been dying to have the opportunity to wear."

The new restaurant on the wharf was packed on a Saturday night. It was a beautiful setting, perched at the edge of the wooden structure with nothing but the water surrounding it. Alyson couldn't help but wonder if the restaurant swayed during the times of the year when the waves were the biggest.

"Did someone think to make reservations?" Alyson asked as she surveyed the hordes of people waiting out front.

"Actually, I did." Devon squeezed his large SUV into a parking space marked compact but was the only one available in the crowded lot. Everyone had to squeeze out the driver's side doors because the car on the passenger side of the vehicle was too close to open the doors more than a crack.

"Sorry about the tight squeeze," Devon said to Trevor's date, Monica, as she tried to maneuver herself from the third row seat without exposing what was under her very short red silk skirt.

"It's not a problem," she mumbled as she tried to balance on the gravel parking area in her three-inch heels.

"Table for six under the name of Stevenson," Devon informed the hostess as the group arrived at the reception desk.

"Yes, this way, sir." The hostess led them to a table in the back of the room, next to a row of windows overlooking the ocean.

"What a great view," Alyson enthused. "How'd you manage to score what is probably the best table in the house?"

"Must be my animal charm." Devon held a chair out for Alyson. "Or it could be the twenty I slipped the hostess when I stopped by earlier to check on the reservation."

"In any case, this is awesome." Alyson leaned over and kissed him on the lips. "You can see the whole bay from here, even the lighthouse on the point. I've been meaning to check out that lighthouse ever since I moved here. It looks really old."

"It is," Mac said. "Haunted too."

"Is everyplace in this town haunted?" Alyson asked.

"Not everywhere, but now that you mention it, we do seem to have more than our share of local spooks. I think it's because this town has such a colorful and sort of violent past. Pirate attacks, the genocide of the indigenous population, lawless settlers from the East, not to mention the slave trade, forced prostitution, and a justice system that included public hangings in the town square."

"I see your point. It's such a great, friendly town now, I guess it's easy to forget about its less-than-savory history. Being new to the area, I guess I'll need to hone up on the area's past."

"My great-uncle's a real history buff," Monica joined in for the first time. "He has hundreds if not thousands of books and original documents related to the history of this whole area. And he loves to talk about it with anyone who will listen. If you're really interested you should give him a call."

"Thank you," Alyson said. "I might do that."

"I'll give you his number, if anyone has a pen I can use."

Alyson dug through her purse for a pen and a scrap of paper. "This is really nice of you. I'm glad Trevor brought you along tonight."

"Your great-uncle doesn't happen to be the old high school librarian, does he?" Mac asked.

"Yeah. He retired three years ago. It almost killed him. He loved that library. How'd you know?"

"I didn't. I just knew that the librarian who retired a few years ago was a local history expert and put two and two together."

"It's a great library," Alyson added. "I could tell that someone who really loved it had designed it."

"He took over as librarian almost fifty years ago, when he was just out of college. Originally, the high school was located in the building where the middle school is now. When they built the new high school my great-uncle designed the library himself. He filled it with some of the books and documents he had collected through the years. It's really quite a collection, but nothing like the one he has at home."

"I'd love to see it sometime. Are you sure your great-uncle wouldn't mind showing it to me?" Alyson asked.

"Are you kidding?" Monica laughed. "I have to warn you, though, that he tends to go on and on if he has an attentive audience. If you still want to go I could set something up."

"We'd love to. Wouldn't we, Mac? You guys want to come along?"

"Yeah, it'd be great," the three responded with differing levels of enthusiasm.

"When do you want to go?" Monica asked the group.

"As soon as possible," Alyson answered enthusiastically.

"Tomorrow's Sunday. I could give him a call to see if he's free."

Everyone agreed that the next day would work for them, so Monica called her great-uncle and set up a meeting for two o'clock the following afternoon. The waitress showed up to take their order just as Monica was finishing her call, and the conversation turned to the excellent seafood the restaurant offered and the evening ahead.

During the movie, Alyson whispered to Devon that he should drop Monica off first so she'd have a chance to talk to the others without her there. It wasn't that she didn't enjoy spending time with her; it was more that she'd decided it was time to tell them about her late-night visitor, and she wasn't sure she was willing to share something like that with someone she didn't know well.

"Something on your mind?" Devon asked after Monica had been safely dropped off at her door.

"Alyson had a rather interesting nocturnal visitor," Mac blurted out.

"A visitor?" Trevor asked.

"A dead one," Mac elaborated.

Alyson filled the guys in on the visit from her late-night guest and the parchment he had led her to.

"Mac and I also found an old journal while we were working at the museum today. It was in a box that held both ancient Indian artifacts as well as some European pieces. The text is handwritten and not readily definable, but it looks a lot like the same language that's on the parchment. I doubt the journal is as old as the parchment, but it looks pretty old, and Mac and I started thinking that maybe the two are related."

"So are we thinking buried treasure?" Trevor leaned over the second-row seat back.

"Maybe."

"Don't tease, Aly. Just the thought of trunks filled with gold and fabulous jewels makes my palms sweat."

"Trevor, I have no more idea about what the parchment or the diary say than you do, but we'll never know if we don't figure out a way to translate them," Alyson pointed out.

"Okay, so what now?" Trevor asked.

"If Monica's great-uncle is as big of an expert on local history as she says he is, he may be able to help us translate both the journal and the parchment,"

Alyson suggested. "The question is, how much do we tell the uncle, or Monica, for that matter? That's why I wanted Devon to drop her off first. We're all in this together; we should decide how much we share and with whom."

"Wow, I don't know." Mac frowned. "How well do you know Monica?" she asked Trevor.

"Not well at all. She's in my English class and she seems nice enough, but I can't say I really know anything about her."

"We have to be careful," Eli joined in for the first time. "We don't know where the parchment, and now the journal, will lead us. We did find a handful of gold coins in the cave. There could be a lot more. If word gets out, everyone and their brother will be wandering around in those caves. Someone could get hurt."

"Yeah, and someone could make off with our treasure," Trevor added.

"Okay, how about this," Devon began, "how about we show the uncle the journal and explain that we got it from the museum, but we don't mention the parchment, cave, or gold coins."

"Makes sense," Alyson agreed. "We could dig around about local history too, to see if we can find out about the caves and how they might have been used to smuggle objects without directly mentioning the caves or what we've found."

"I have an uncle of my own who likes to talk, and usually once you get people like that going they tell you everything about everything until you stop them," Mac offered. "We probably just need to ask a general question about smugglers and we'll get the whole scoop."

"Okay, I'll pick everyone up tomorrow at around twelve thirty and we'll have a bite and come up with a strategy," Devon suggested.

"Sounds like a plan," Alyson agreed. "And I'll call the woman who donated the journal in the morning to see if I can get any more details about its history."

Chapter 5

Sunday morning left no doubt that winter had officially arrived. The days had been getting shorter and the nights colder for a few weeks, but this morning everything was covered in frost, making the landscape around the old house on the clifftop look like a fairyland. At least the central heating/air-conditioning system that had been part of the old house's major remodel had finally been hooked up the week before, so there was warm air pumping through the vents at that very minute. Up until just a few short days earlier Alyson and her mom had had to rely solely on the warmth provided by the house's nine fireplaces for heat. Alyson loved her bedroom fireplace and stoked up a fire most nights, but it was nice to wake up to the instant heat provided by forced air in the morning.

"Do you need to go out?" Alyson asked Tucker.

He thumped his tale once in response but didn't get up from his curled-up position on the rug by her bed.

"A bit lazy today, aren't we?"

Tucker lifted his head from his paws and whined in response.

"Come on; let's get this over with," Alyson said, digging around in the closet for her rattiest pair of running shoes. "It's freezing this morning and I think Mom's making bacon for breakfast. I can smell it frying."

One thing Alyson loved most about her mom was her amazing cooking ability. Mornings always started with a hot meal, not some cold cereal or boring toast.

"I'm taking Tucker for a run," Alyson called to her mother as she let Tucker out the front door and into the frigid morning air. Alyson loved to run along the clifftops overlooking the Pacific Ocean. In spite of the chilly air, the sun shone brightly, reflecting off the rolling surf below.

Alyson settled into a rhythm, the steady sound of her own feet against the damp earth her only music. After several minutes of running, she headed inland slightly, until she found herself at the base of the cliff face, where she and the gang had found the entrance to the cave that had housed the gold coins, as well as an old trunk that had helped them solve a mystery and a very dead body.

Alyson hesitated, then climbed the cliff face and slipped inside. The large cavern was dark, with only the dim glow from the small entrance to light the way. Alyson looked around but couldn't see much without a flashlight. Tucker panted beside her.

"It's okay, boy. We'll go. I don't know why I even came down here."

She had turned to climb back through the narrow opening just as she heard a scream and a crash from somewhere beyond the reach of the light.

"Who's there?" she yelled, grabbing Tucker's collar to keep him from running toward the sound.

Her inquiry was met with silence. The scream seemed to have come from a man. It sounded far away, somewhere in the tunnels beyond the main room. Alyson hesitated and looked at Tucker. He seemed unconcerned, as if he hadn't heard what she had. He wagged his tail as he sat next to her. She must have imagined it. Maybe she was losing her mind after all.

After showering and dressing in comfortable cords and a warm sweater, Alyson went down to the kitchen for breakfast. There was a fire crackling merrily in the brick fireplace at the end of the room, and golden omelets, crispy bacon, and fluffy homemade biscuits were waiting on cobalt blue plates when she arrived.

"Coffee?" her mom asked, setting a matching blue mug on the polished oak table.

"Sure, and some juice too, if you have it."

"How was your run?"

"Cold but nice. I really love it here. More than I could have imagined when we moved here. Can you believe it's only been three months? It seems like a lot longer."

"A lot has happened in those three months," her mom reminded her. "You've already had more adventure here than most people have in a lifetime."

"Speaking of adventure, we might have found someone to help us translate the journal we found yesterday." Alyson filled her mother in on Monica's great-uncle and their plan to pay him a visit later in the day.

"Were you able to get any information from the woman who donated the journal?"

"By the time Mac and I finished all the slave labor you assigned us yesterday we didn't have time to call her," Alyson teased. "I thought I'd call her this morning. Do you know anything about her?"

"No, I've never met her. I could ask around, though."

"Maybe," Alyson mumbled with her mouth full of a light, fluffy biscuit dripping with melted butter and fresh boysenberry jam. She wiped a drop of jam from her chin with the back of her hand. "I'll let you know. If I can get hold of her today I may not need you to go to all that trouble."

"It's no trouble. I'm at the museum every day anyway. The opening is in less than two weeks. I'm really excited about it."

"The place looks great. You, Caleb, and the men and women of the historical society should be proud."

"We are. Thanks." Her mother got up and poured herself another cup of coffee. "Do you want to grab some dinner tonight? Just the two of us? It's been a long time since we've shared a quiet meal together."

"I'd love to. Let's say around seven. That should give me plenty of time to meet with Monica's uncle, hang with the gang for a bit, and get cleaned up. I'd die for Italian. We haven't done Italian in forever. How about Alfredo's downtown?"

"Italian sounds great."

After finishing every last bite of her delicious meal, Alyson stacked her dishes in the dishwasher and went upstairs to make her call.

As promised, Devon picked everyone up at around twelve thirty and they headed over to Pirates Pizza, where they managed to snag their regular booth in the corner. After ordering several large Pirates Combos, they settled in to discuss their strategy for the upcoming meeting with Monica's uncle.

"Let's hope he can help us figure out the language and find the treasure," Eli said as the piping hot pizzas were delivered to the table.

"So how much do we tell him?" Trevor asked as he took a slice for himself. "Last night we talked about showing him the journal but not the parchment. Won't he think it's strange that a bunch of high school kids would give up their Sunday just to translate some old journal?"

"That's true," Eli acknowledged. "If it wasn't for the parchment and the possibility of buried treasure I certainly wouldn't be interested in some old journal."

"We could say we're researching the journal on behalf of the museum," Alyson suggested. "And that the historical society really wanted to be able to provide a history and possibly a partial translation as part of the exhibit."

"Maybe we're overthinking this," Devon interrupted. "If the old guy is in to history as much as everyone says he is, it may not seem strange to him at all that someone else shares his interest. I say we just engage in conversation, see what he knows, and take it from there."

"Devon's right," Mac agreed. "We've already agreed not to mention the parchment, coins, or cave at this point; beyond that, let's just take it as it comes."

After devouring all three of the pizzas they'd ordered, they picked up Monica and headed over to her great-uncle's seaside estate. The house was a large, two-story colonial with single-story wings on either side, built of red brick.

"Wow, librarians must make a ton of money," Trevor said in awe as Devon pulled the Expedition into the circular drive.

"Hardly." Monica laughed. "My great-uncle comes from old money on his mother's side. His job with the school district had more to do with a love of books than the need for a salary. In fact, I think he donated most, if not all, of the money that built the high school library."

Alyson unbuckled her seat belt and stepped onto the gravel driveway. "The house is beautiful. It looks like something you'd find in Beverly Hills, not Cutter's Cove, Oregon."

"I'll give you a tour after you meet my uncle," Monica offered. "I'm sure he won't mind. He may offer to do it himself. He loves to show off all the furniture and artwork he's collected in his travels."

The group walked up the seven steps to the front door and rang the bell. A tall, thin woman in a tidy maid's uniform let them in. "Monica," she said, hugging her warmly. "It's been so long since you've come to visit."

"I know, Maggie. I've been busy with school and stuff. We'll catch up later, but Uncle Rory is expecting us. These are my friends," she said, introducing each one in turn. "They're here to talk with him about local history."

"He'll love that." Maggie smiled. "A fair warning, though: Once you get him started you may not be able to get him to stop. I think I saw him head toward the library a little while ago. Follow me."

The group followed the maid through the entry, past a grand staircase leading to the second floor, through a large living area with vaulted ceilings and a floor-to-ceiling fireplace, down a hall lined with artwork, and into a room that was even more charming than the library at the high school.

"Uncle Rory," Monica greeted a jolly-looking man.

"These are the friends I was telling you about." Again, she introduced each by name.

"Please call me Booker."

"Is that your last name?" Alyson asked.

"No, it's a nickname I picked up in college. My dorm mates started calling me Booker because I always had my head in a book. It just kind of stuck."

"Not a bad nickname as nicknames go," Trevor commented. "I know a guy who wet his pants on the first day of kindergarten and has been known as Pisser ever since."

"Oh, that's cruel." Booker laughed. "So, Monica tells me you're interested in learning about our local history."

"We are," Alyson confirmed. "It's really nice of you to take time out of your weekend to meet with us."

"I'm always happy to make time for fellow history buffs," he said, indicating that they should make themselves comfortable on the overstuffed leather sofas in the center of the large room, grouped around hardwood tables.

The high-ceilinged room was somewhat similar to the library at the high school, though much larger; unlike the library at school, it boasted a large brick fireplace that added warmth and coziness. Thousands of books were arranged on mahogany shelves arranged on all four walls on two levels. The shelves on the first level were about six feet tall, and there were two sets of stairs, one on either end of the room, leading to the second-level stacks. Most spectacular of all, tucked into a large bay window overlooking the rocky shoreline and the Pacific Ocean, sat a grand old desk and a red leather chair.

"Is there anything specific you're interested in? A particular time period maybe?"

Alyson was the first to speak. "I'm sure you've heard that the historical society is opening a museum downtown in a couple of weeks."

"Yes indeed. I'm a member of the society myself, but I've been in Europe for the past several months and haven't had a chance to check things out yet. I just got home last week and have been meaning to stop by sometime in the next few days."

"My mom is one of the founders of the museum," Alyson informed him. "Mac and I were there yesterday, helping to unpack and catalogue things, when we came across a journal. It got us talking about Cutter's Cove's past and started us wondering who might have written the journal and what it might say."

"Did you bring it with you?" Booker asked.

"Yes, it's in my handbag." Alyson dug into her bag and pulled out the leather-bound volume. She handed it to the kindly librarian.

He opened the book and thumbed through it. After a few minutes he walked over to a bookshelf and lifted a heavy volume from one of the shelves. He opened the book and turned to the index. He found what he was looking for and turned to a page in the middle of the book and started to read.

"Interesting. Very interesting. You've got quite a find here. Quite a find indeed."

"What is it?" Alyson asked.

"The journal seems to be written in a hybrid language known as Chinook jargon."

"You don't happen to read Chinook jargon, do you?" Mac asked hopefully.

"No, I'm afraid I don't. It was a short-lived language that became extinct long before my time."

"Why?" Trevor asked.

"There are a couple of things that led to its demise. It was a trade language that developed between the early settlers and the natives as a way to bridge the communication gap. Its roots were based in Chinook, but there were words borrowed from French, English, and other indigenous languages. As more Europeans settled in this area, they brought European diseases such as smallpox and malaria, and by the turn of the century most of the native population had died off. With the extinction of the native people in the area, the need for a language that bridged the gap between the cultures diminished."

"That's so sad," Alyson whispered.

"Do you know of anyone who might be able to read the language today?" Devon asked, referring back to the journal Booker still held.

"No, I'm afraid I don't. I do, however, have some old texts that provide a partial translation, sort of a cheat sheet to Chinook jargon. It by no means provides a complete dictionary, but you might be able to translate enough of the words to figure out the gist of the journal. I'll let you borrow it if you promise to be very careful with it."

"That would be great," Alyson said. "I'll let you know what the journal says if I can manage to figure it out."

Booker looked on a bookshelf for a moment, then returned with a leather pouch filled with single sheets of handwritten material. The paper had yellowed with age but the writing seemed clear, and Alyson hoped there was enough information there to translate both the journal and the parchment.

"If you kids want a tour of the house I'll fill you in on some of Cutter's Cove's more interesting ancestors while we look around. The town really does have quite a colorful past."

"Speaking of colorful characters," Monica said, "Alyson recently moved into the Cutter house."

"You must be the young lady who found out old Barkley had a grandson. That was a good piece of detective work, my dear."

"Thanks, but I can't take all the credit. It was really a group effort. I never could have found Caleb without everyone's help."

"If you just moved in to the Cutter house, your mom must be the cute blonde Charlie was going on and on about." Booker took Alyson's hand and began to walk toward the hall. "He's quite a player, that Charlie, and he's got a real thing for your mother. I'd keep an eye on him."

Alyson smiled. "I'll do that." She knew who Charlie was. He'd been helping out at the museum for weeks. He was a sweet old guy, and a bit of a flirt, but a good thirty years older than her mother.

The interior of the house turned out to be as magnificent as the exterior, and Booker's narration was both funny and fascinating. Alyson really liked Booker. He was charming and smart and, quite frankly, a bit of a flirt himself. After thanking him for the tour and promising to return the papers soon, the gang climbed back into the Expedition for the short trip back to town.

After Alyson returned from dinner with her mother, she spent the rest of the evening trying to translate the journal. Between her own knowledge of English and French and the helpful guide Booker had provided, she was able to translate enough of the text that she could begin to make out a few passages. It seemed that the Native American who wrote the journal had a close relationship with one or more European traders. There were references to men in ships. Both the word *man* and the word *ship* were the same as the English words. There were also direct translations for father (*papa*), mother (*mama*), sail, sick, help, sun, moon, and week, among others.

After identifying words with a direct English-to-Chinook-jargon translation, Alyson put her expensive private school education to work and identified as many French-to-Chinook-jargon words as she could find. That alone helped her to translate some entire sentences.

The writer of the journal spoke of men coming in ships, trading goods, and kissing native girls. The pages also spoke of sickness and disease and, most interestingly, some sort of curse following the theft of a sacred object. There was a reference to something called a *tumtumtamahnos*. She'd have to ask Booker if he knew what that referred to.

Alyson put on the tank top and boxer shorts she slept in and turned off the lights. She was exhausted. As she faded away into the world of dreams she thought she heard a voice whisper, "Beware of the curse."

Chapter 6

The next day a very tired Alyson filled the others in on her progress at lunch. By the time she had finished translating what she could of the journal it had been only a couple of hours before it was time to get up for school, so the only thing keeping Alyson awake at that point was massive amounts of caffeine.

"So I figured," she concluded after telling her story, "that maybe there's a local legend concerning the missing or stolen object, and who better to ask than Booker? I was hoping Monica would join us for lunch today so I could ask her for his phone number."

"I'll see if I can get it for you when I see her next period," Trevor promised. "But what I'm more interested in is whether you were able to translate the parchment."

"No, I'm afraid I didn't get to it. I got really wrapped up in the journal, and before I knew it I only had a couple of hours to sleep before I had to get ready for school."

"I'm with Trevor," Eli said. "I'm much more interested in the parchment. How about we get together after football practice to see if we can figure it out? We can meet in the library."

"I guess that would be okay," Alyson agreed reluctantly. "The material Booker gave me to use in translating the material is at home, though. I'll have to go get it."

"I'll go with you, and while we're out we can stop by to ask Booker about the missing sacred object," Mac suggested.

Later that afternoon, Mac and Alyson pulled up in the driveway outside Booker's beautiful home. Neither of them was completely certain Trevor had asked Monica to call her uncle to ask him whether it was okay for them to stop by.

"I hope he doesn't mind that we're just dropping by," Alyson said nervously.

"I guess we'll find out soon enough."

Maggie answered the door once again and immediately asked them to come in. "Monica called to say we'd be seeing you again."

"Oh, good." The girls followed the maid into the entry hall. "I wasn't sure if Trevor was able to talk to her. I apologize for just showing up like this."

Maggie smiled. "You're quite welcome any time. The mister is always happy to talk history with anyone who will listen. He's waiting for you in his study. I'll show you the way."

The study was a much smaller room in the same wing of the house as the library. It held a desk and chair, a computer station complete with a printer, several file cabinets, and a small sofa covered in deep green fabric. There were no windows in the room, but a large saltwater aquarium added light and life to the room.

"Why don't we go across the hall to the library?" Booker suggested. "This room is a bit small, but it's secure, with no outside entry, so I keep my investment and research materials here."

"We're really sorry to interrupt you," Alyson started off. "But I translated some large portions of the journal last night that left me with some questions."

"I'm always happy to have visitors." Booker indicated that they should sit down on one of the leather sofas. "This big old house gets pretty lonely sometimes. It's just Maggie and me most days, although the gardener does come around on Mondays and Fridays, and he usually stops in for a cold one. Now, what can I do for you?"

Alyson pulled out the journal and showed Booker what she had translated so far. "What I'm most curious about is the reference to *tumtumtamahnos*. Do you have any idea what they might be?"

Booker stood up and walked over to one of his bookshelves to find a particular volume. He pulled down a large old text and began to look through the pages. "That does sound familiar. I seem to remember something about a local legend surrounding a sacred object."

He flipped through a few more pages. "Here it is. The native people in this region believed in the protective power of a life spirit that nurtured and protected the area. It was known as Tumtumtamahnos, a gold statue with a large emerald in its forehead. It was said that as long as Tumtumtamahnos protected the river valley, the area would prosper, the crops would flourish, and the people would be healthy and happy. The statue was kept in a shrine somewhere, probably in one of the underground caverns. The people of the river valley worshipped it, offering sacrifices to it in return for its continued protection."

Booker adjusted his glasses and continued to read. "Sometime after the first Europeans settled in the area the statue was stolen. Many believed it was taken by one of the settlers; others thought a local native stole it to offer in trade to the settlers. In any event, after it disappeared from its sacred shrine the people of the river valley started getting sick and dying. Most of the natives believed it was because of the disappearance of the statue, but history shows that the timing of the theft coincided with major outbreaks of smallpox and malaria brought by the Europeans. The native people had no immunity to even the most minor of these diseases and the result was catastrophic."

"Did they ever recover the statue?" Alyson asked.

"No, it's never been seen again. Which in and of itself is interesting. Even in those days, most stolen objects showed up at some point. Some historians believe that whoever stole it made it part of a private collection and has never been put up for sale. Others have suggested that the emerald was removed and the gold melted down for its monetary value. Still others are certain the statue never left this area—that whoever stole it hid it somewhere in the cavern system and there it remains today.

"The reality is," Booker continued, "we may never know what really happened to it unless it shows up at some point in the future. Personally, I hope whoever stole it hid it or added it to a private collection. It would be a tragedy if a piece of such historical significance was simply melted down."

"Yes, it would be. Thanks so much for your time." Alyson got up and started toward the door. "If it's all right with you, I'd like to keep your translation materials another day or two. I'll bring them back by the end of the week."

"That's fine, dear. Keep them as long as you'd like."

Alyson and Mac met the rest of the gang in the school library as planned. As usual for that time of day, the place was deserted except for the presence of the librarian, who was busy sorting books behind the counter. They rolled the parchment out on a large table near the local history section. On one side was crude writing, as if someone had hastily jotted down a message with whatever writing implement was available. On the other was expertly drafted calligraphy, something that probably could only be produced using the finest writing instruments of the time.

"The finely written side is a ship's manifest in some form of Spanish. Probably a local dialect," Mac informed them.

"So our mystery author comes to Cutter's Cove to trade goods, and while he's here he has a need to write something down and uses the back of the manifest?" Eli asked.

"The evidence would seem to point to that conclusion," Mac confirmed.

"But why the two different languages?" Trevor asked.

"It could be that the author of the writing on the back intended the message for someone from this area who wouldn't be able to read Spanish," Mac hypothesized.

"Makes sense," Trevor said. "Do you think the parchment is written in the same language as the journal?"

"It's hard to tell, but Chinook jargon is as good a place as any to start," Devon said. "Let's compare what we have to the translations Booker lent us and we'll see what we come up with."

They spent the next couple of hours comparing the hastily written words on the back of the parchment with the sample of the language provided by Booker's text and the partially translated journal and eventually had a partial translation.

"It looks like a riddle," Mac observed.

"The message was obviously meant for a specific audience," Alyson agreed. "Someone who would understand the significance of the clues."

"It could be the directions to a meeting place to exchange goods between the sea captain and the local people." Trevor stood up and paced around the table. "Really, at this point we have nothing. Even if we manage to translate the entire text and figure out the clues, we have no way of knowing if they'll lead us to anything. The trade could have been completed back in 1826 or thereabouts and there may be nothing to find."

"I wonder if there's a record of the *Santa Inez*," Mac said. "It might be interesting to find out exactly when the ship was here and if there were any strange occurrences that coincide with its arrival. I could check online tonight, but honestly, I think our best bet might be Booker. He seems to have a lot of resources about local history."

"He gave me his cell phone number when we were there this afternoon. I can call him to see if he's ever heard of the ship," Alyson volunteered. "The thing is, at some point he's going to start to wonder what we're up to. First we have all these questions about the journal. Then we start asking about merchant ships from the eighteen hundreds. Let's face it: The further we get into this, the more questions we're going to come up with. Maybe we should just be straight with him. He seems pretty honest and trustworthy to me, and he doesn't seem like the type to go blabbing our secrets all over town."

"You might have a point," Mac agreed. "It really does seem like he might be a huge help to us. He has access to original documents we'll never find on the Internet."

"I'm not sure we should bring up the parchment over the phone. Maybe we should call him to see if we could meet with him tomorrow," Alyson said.

"I promised to help my dad work on his latest software program," Devon informed them.

"Eli and I will have football practice all afternoon," Trevor added. "If we win our game on Friday we're in the state finals, so Coach is working us really hard."

"How about you, Mac? Want to come?" Alyson asked.

"Sure. Maybe you could pick me up at Cybertech on your way. That way I won't have to come back to campus."

"How's your work program going anyway?" Alyson asked. "It must be interesting to work with such advanced software."

"It's really fun. And challenging. And it's kind of nice to be able to leave school after lunch. It's like having a real job except I don't get paid. But getting college credits while I'm still in high school will really help me when I apply for college admission."

"Like you aren't already going to be accepted to pretty much every college in the known world anyway," Alyson teased. "With your test scores and references, you should be able to go pretty much anywhere you want."

"Yeah, I guess. But college is still a couple of years away, and I plan to focus on having the whole high school experience."

"Maybe we could meet at the Cannery after football practice," Trevor suggested. "We could get a bite to eat and go over what, if anything, you learn from Booker. And I heard they got a new DJ this week who plays a lot of alternative stuff. I've been wanting to stop by anyway."

"Sounds fine with me," Alyson agreed.

"Me too," Devon confirmed.

"I'll have to check with my mom," Mac added.

"Sounds like a plan." Eli started gathering his books and other supplies as the librarian started shutting down computers for the evening. "I think we're about to get kicked out of here anyway."

Alyson took Tucker out for a quick run as soon as she got home, then joined her mother for dinner in their newly remodeled kitchen. Tucker curled up on the braided rug in front of the crackling fire while Alyson set the table.

"Our new dining room table came in today," Alyson's mom informed her as she spooned thick, creamy clam chowder into large soup bowls. "I'm having it delivered tomorrow."

"That's great, Mom." Alyson broke off a piece of the hot French bread that had just come out of the oven. She slathered a large portion of the fresh butter her mom bought from a local dairy every week over its surface and set it on her plate next to a generous portion of crisp green salad.

"I hope you don't mind, but I asked Mac and her family, and Devon and Eli and their father, to

Thanksgiving dinner. I plan to ask Trevor too, if he's not doing anything with his family, but I haven't had a chance to do it yet," Alyson informed her mom.

"No, that's fine. We bought that great big table; we might as well break it in."

"Mac's mom is going to call you to see if they can bring something." Alyson took a large spoonful of the thick chowder. "It'll be nice to have a big crowd for the holiday. I was afraid it was going to be just the two of us. Not that I don't love hanging out with you, but holidays should be noisy."

"I agree. I'm glad you invited them. I really like your friends. I'd like to meet their parents. I'm sure they're really good people. People you can trust and rely on."

"Um, Mom—" Alyson set her spoon down and smoothed the napkin on her lap. "I sort of have something to talk to you about. It involves those trusty, reliable friends. At least, it involves Mac."

Alyson explained the set of circumstances that led to her sharing her secret with Mac. She knew her mom wouldn't be happy about the situation, but she didn't want to lie to her either.

"Oh, Alyson." She sighed.

"I know I promised I wouldn't tell anyone, but I trust Mac, and lying to her hasn't felt right for a very long time."

"And the others?" her mom asked.

"Mac promised she'd never tell anyone. No one else knows, not Trevor or Devon or anyone. She knows how serious this is. I know she'll keep our secret."

Sarah Prescott sat quietly for a minute. "I trust Mac, I really do, but Aly, you know how precarious our situation is. If word got out, I'm not sure I could keep you safe. Amanda Parker is dead. We need to keep it that way."

Chapter 7

Alyson took her seat beside Mac in first period the next morning. She'd tossed and turned for most of the night, going over everything in her mind again and again. It would be a miracle if she was able to stay awake in class.

"Our meeting with Booker is all set for this afternoon," she whispered. "He seemed excited that we were so interested in local history. He said he found out some more information about Tumtumtamahnos that he seemed excited to share with us."

"What are you two whispering about up there?" Chelsea asked from the table she shared with Trevor directly behind the pair. "You're not involved in some new mystery, are you? Because the last thing we need with the big game just a few days away is some big distraction. The cheerleaders have been working really hard and we deserve to have everyone's full attention."

"Uh, what about the football team?" Mac asked, turning around to face the two behind them. "Don't you think maybe they're the ones who deserve everyone's attention?"

"Well, them too of course, but everyone knows the football team would be nothing without the cheerleaders to cheer them on. Right, Trev?"

"Sure, Chelsea. The cheerleaders rule."

Chelsea smiled smugly at Mac. "See, I told you so."

"Typical Chelsea," Mac groaned as she turned around to face the front of the room. "Totally clueless in Chelsealand."

"I heard that, Mackenzie Reynolds."

"So, are you guys ready for Friday's game?" Alyson asked Trevor, changing the subject.

"I think so. We're playing really well, but Portsmouth is a good team. They'll be tough to beat. Coach is really riding us hard this week. I'm not sure how much Eli and I will be able to help with…"

Alyson cleared her throat and looked toward Chelsea.

"With the thing for the museum," Trevor improvised.

"Don't even get me started on that," Chelsea jumped in. "I tried to talk Caleb into going to Sun Valley with my family over Thanksgiving, but he wouldn't even consider it because his precious museum opening is the day before. I don't see why anyone would choose some stuffy old museum over skiing on fresh powder with yours truly."

"Chelsea," Alyson reminded her, "Caleb is one of the founding members of the new museum. He donated the building that houses it. Of course he'd want to be there. It's a really big day for him. Besides, why do you want him to go skiing with you anyway? You're not even that good friends, are you?"

"Sure we are. I helped out with that Halloween thing and everything. Besides, I figured he'd be fun to have along, seeing how he has all that money just waiting to be spent. Sun Valley has excellent shopping."

"And you figure he should spend it on you?"

"Why not? He sure isn't spending it on himself. I mean, he inherited all that money almost two months ago and he's still wearing the same ratty old clothes he's always worn."

"I heard he bought a new truck," Alyson defended her friend.

"Used truck," Chelsea corrected. "Who buys a used truck when they can afford a new Ferrari? The boy seriously needs some guidance. If he wants to date me, he's going to have to do better than some old Ford F-150."

"I didn't know he wanted to date you," Mac commented.

"Of course he wants to date me; everyone wants to date me."

"Oh, please," Mac groaned.

"You're just jealous because I can have any guy I want and you're destined to die a lonely old woman with a house full of cats."

"Hello. Dating the star wide receiver," Mac reminded her.

"For now," Chelsea drawled.

"So," Alyson intervened, before a full-fledged catfight broke out, "what are you doing for Thanksgiving, Trevor?"

"Probably nothing. My family is going to my grandparents' in Idaho, but if we win the game on Friday I'll have practice next week. The state finals are only two weeks away."

"In that case, you're invited to my house. Mac and her family, and Devon, Eli, and his dad are coming. It should be a good time."

"Thanks, I'd like that. Your mom's excellent cooking is definitely a step up from the frozen turkey dinner I was planning to have."

"Can I have your attention?" Mr. Harris interrupted. Alyson and Mac turned around to face the front of the room. "The instructions for today's lab are being passed out. Please read them very carefully and follow the directions exactly. I don't want a repeat performance of last year's incident."

"What happened last year?" Alyson whispered.

"Let's just say the school had to be evacuated, Todd Brown's eyebrows were permanently burned off, and the science room had to be completely remodeled. I'll tell you the whole story later. It's really quite funny," Mac whispered back.

After school Alyson picked up Mac and headed over to Booker's for the third day in a row. When they pulled into the circular drive they saw him pruning roses near the front entry.

"I thought you said you had a gardener." Alyson climbed out of the front seat of her vehicle and joined him.

"I do, but sometimes I like to come out here and get a little dirty myself. I'm getting too old to engage in a lot of the outdoor pursuits I used to, but gardening is a way to keep me close to nature."

"I hope we're not interrupting," Alyson apologized.

"No, no. You're always welcome. Did you make some more headway on the journal?"

"No, and that's not why we're here." Alyson looked around. "Is there somewhere we could sit and talk?"

"Let's go into the library. It's getting a little nippy out here anyway."

Alyson and Mac followed their host through a side door and into the library.

"Make yourself at home. I'm going to go wash up and see if Maggie can bring us some coffee."

Booker headed out the door and Alyson sat down on one of the large sofas. Mac went over to the closest bookshelf and randomly pulled out a book.

"Isn't this library great?" She opened the book in her hand. "To have all these books available to you all the time. I can't even imagine how wonderful that must be. I wonder if he's read them all."

"I doubt it," Alyson said. "There must be thousands of books in here. It would take a lifetime to read all of them."

"Well, he *is* called Booker."

"Good point. But still, it sounds like he also travels and has friends and stuff. And he did work as a librarian for something like forty years. Chances are most of these books were bought as part of a collection. A lot of people collect books as a hobby or for investment purposes."

"Coffee is on the way." Booker came into the room and took a seat opposite Alyson. "What can I do for you kids today?"

"Well," Alyson started, "when we were here the other day we didn't exactly tell you everything." She shifted nervously in her seat. "You remember how we were looking for Barkley Cutter's heir a few months ago?"

"Sure, I remember. You uncovered a grandson."

"Well, during the search we found these." Alyson set the gold coins on the table between them.

Booker picked up one of the coins and looked at it in amazement. "Where did you find these?"

"They were in a cave near my house. Actually, my dog found the cave. The opening is really small and hidden, but Tucker managed to find his way in and when we went in after him we found these, as well as the key to an old trunk that helped us solve the mystery of Barkley's missing grandson. Oh, and there was also a dead body."

"A dead body?"

"Well, a skeleton. It looked like it had been there a really long time. We think it might have been one of the sailors who used to come through Cutter's Cove to exchange goods with the Native Americans."

"And we found a gold medallion near the skeleton that said *Santa Inez* on the back. And this parchment," Alyson added.

They'd decided it was best to let Booker believe the parchment had been in the cave with the other items. There was no way they wanted to try to explain Alyson's ghostly visitor.

"Well I'll be." Booker unrolled the parchment and carefully examined both sides.

"We think the front is a ship's manifest," Mac offered.

"And the back of the document?" Booker asked.

"It seems to be in Chinook jargon," Alyson explained. "We've done a partial translation, but so far we haven't been able to figure out enough to understand the message. It appears to be some sort of riddle."

Booker looked at the document more carefully. "I think you might be right."

"We think someone simply used the back of the manifest to record something they wanted to be sure someone locally could read. Otherwise why not just use the same language as was used on the front?"

"Makes sense." Booker got up from the sofa and wandered over to a bookcase. "If this manifest was in the possession of the person who wrote the words on the back, it must have been someone of high rank, probably the captain. I wonder what would be so important that the captain of a ship would write on the back of such a document. And, more importantly, why was it in the cave?"

"It might not have been in the cave originally." Alyson sat forward on the sofa.

"Sounds like you have quite a mystery," Booker said. "I love a good mystery. I really want to thank you kids for trusting me enough to let me in on this. And don't worry; for now, this is our little secret."

Booker grabbed a couple of old leather pouches from the top of one of the shelves. "I seem to remember reading an account of the *Santa Inez* and its visit to Cutter's Cove somewhere. I've been collecting old clippings, letters, diaries, and what-not for years. I'm sure there's something in here."

Booker opened the first pouch and hundreds of pieces of yellowed paper came spilling out. "This may take a while to go through. Maybe I should look through this stuff later and get back to you tomorrow. For now, though, let's see if there's any official record of the ship's manifest on file."

Booker wandered back over to the bookshelf and climbed up on the ladder near the second-level stacks. "Can you give me a hand?"

Mac got up and climbed the short flight of stairs to the second story. "What do you need?"

"There's a large volume on the second to the top shelf. I'm afraid it's a bit heavy for me to lift down and it's very old, so I don't want to risk dropping it. The gray one with the torn binding."

Mac took the book down, then carried it down the stairs and set it on the table next to the gold coins and parchment. She opened the front cover. "When was this printed?"

"Sometime around the mid-to-late nineteenth century. It's a description of the ships that sailed during the late–seventeen hundreds through the mid–eighteen hundreds. There's a brief history of each, a listing of the cargo they carried, the names of the crew, and their status as of the publication of the book."

Booker carefully thumbed through the delicate pages. "Here we are. The *Santa Inez* was a merchant ship that sailed from Ecuador along the West Coast to Alaska and back in the early eighteen hundreds. Its cargo included coffee and tobacco from the south and furs, leather, and wood from the north. There's also a reference to an unsanctioned use of the ship to transport slaves along the coast. The ships final voyage was in 1826."

"What happened to it?" Mac asked.

Booker continued to read. "It appears that part of the crew mutinied during the passage home. The ship was badly damaged during the battle, but it managed to make port somewhere along the Baja Peninsula. The remaining crew found jobs on other ships and the local government confiscated the ship's cargo."

"Why did the crew mutiny?" Alyson asked.

"This book doesn't really say." Booker turned the page and read to the end of the section on the *Santa Inez*. "I'll do some further research and see what I can find out."

"The dead guy in the cave seems to have been from the *Santa Inez*," Alyson pointed out. "Maybe whatever conflict that caused the crew to mutiny at sea started here."

"Yeah," Mac agreed. "Maybe the ship's captain was the one who stole the statue. If the skeleton in the cave was the captain, maybe someone from the crew figured out what he did and killed him before the ship ever left here. Or maybe he arranged to smuggle the statue out of the area for someone else. It sounds like it had a very significant monetary value as well as its importance as a sacred object."

"There seem to be a lot of things that may or may not be related." Alyson sat forward on the sofa. "The missing sacred object, the writing on the back of the parchment, the mutiny of the crew. We need to see if we can find anything that definitively links them. Right now all we really have is speculation."

"I'll keep looking and maybe we should meet again tomorrow," Booker said. "I have a lot of original documents from the time period involved, and if something really significant happened I'm sure there must be a record of it somewhere."

"I can come back here after school tomorrow. Around three o'clock," Alyson said.

"I'm in too," Mac added.

"That would be fine. I'll have Maggie prepare some of her world-famous scones. They're really quite delightful. You simply must try them."

"I'll work on translating more of the parchment tonight." Alyson rolled up the yellowed document. "Maybe if we can figure out exactly what it says it will give us a clue to the rest of the mystery."

She stood up and started gathering her things. "Uh, Booker, have you heard anything about a curse attached to the sacred statue?"

"No; why do you ask?" Booker asked just as a loud crash sounded in the hallway.

"What was that?" Mac gasped.

Booker walked to the door and looked into the hall. "Are you all right?"

"I thought the door was closed," Alyson whispered to Mac.

"It was just Maggie," Booker explained. "She dropped a serving tray."

"Okay, then, we'll be on our way." Alyson left the library and headed toward the front door.

"Do you think Maggie was listening to us?" Mac asked as they started down the driveway.

"I don't know. I could swear Booker closed the door when we went in, but when he went to check on the noise in the hall it was open."

"Maybe Maggie left it open when she brought the coffee."

"Maybe."

Chapter 8

Trevor, Eli, and Devon were sitting at a large table near the dance floor when the others arrived at the Cannery. Trevor was talking to the cute blond waitress who had served them the other night. She sat perched on the corner of the table near his arm and was laughing at something he had said.

"Isn't she a little old for him?" Mac mumbled under her breath. "I didn't know this place employed cradle-robbing waitresses."

"Sheath the claws, Mac." Alyson put her arm through Mac's. "She's probably just taking his order."

"Order for what? It doesn't look like either one of them has chili cheese burgers or nitro wings on their mind."

"Wave to Eli," Alyson coached her friend. "He's going to wonder why you're glaring at Trevor instead of acknowledging him. He's been looking at you since we walked in the door."

Mac smiled at Eli and sat down on the plastic chair next to him. "Been here long?" she asked.

"About twenty minutes." Eli leaned over to kiss her on the cheek. "We waited to order food until you got here, but I'm starved, so I hope you guys know what you want."

After everyone had ordered and the waitress had gone to wait on another table they settled in to catch up on their day.

"Practice was brutal," Trevor complained, rubbing his throwing arm. "If Coach doesn't back off a little he's going to wear everyone out before the game on Friday. I saw Rick Lightener limping as he walked to his car after practice. He's our best running back. I hope Coach knows what he's doing."

"You're the team captain," Alyson pointed out. "Maybe you should have a talk with him."

"Somehow I don't envision that conversation going very well at all. Coach seems really tense now that our going to state seems like a real possibility. We only have two more practices before the game. I'm sure we can tough it out."

"So how'd you guys do?" Eli asked. "Was Booker helpful in translating the parchment or filling in the blanks concerning the *Santa Inez*?"

Alyson and Mac filled them in on the details of the afternoon.

"We're planning to go back to Booker's house again tomorrow afternoon," Alyson finished up. "Hopefully he'll have more information about the missing relic and the mutiny of the *Santa Inez*."

"Do you think the two things are related?" Trevor asked Alyson.

"I don't know. Maybe. There seem to have been a lot of things going on around the same time. I'm going to try to translate some more of the parchment if I can get my homework done in time. Maybe the message on the back will provide some clues or help fill in some of the blanks."

"I hope it's a treasure map," Eli said enthusiastically "Maybe it will even lead us to the missing statue. Or more of those gold coins we found. Either way, I'm envisioning a significant boost to my financial status."

"You do realize," Alyson cautioned, "that even if the writing does turn out to be some sort of map, there's no guarantee any treasure will still be there. The paper is almost two hundred years old. A lot can happen in two hundred years."

"Yeah, but maybe there's a treasure still hidden just waiting for us to find it. Stranger things have happened, and our track record at finding missing objects is adding up in the plus column."

"You might be right," Alyson granted. "Either way, it's a search worth pursuing, so I say we keep working on it and see where it takes us. Right now I need to get home to start working on the homework that's been piling up this week. Let's get together to talk at lunch tomorrow."

"Sounds like a plan." Trevor got up and started gathering his things. "Can I bum a ride? I left my car at school, and I'm not sure my legs are working well enough for me to walk back there to pick it up."

"You guys almost lost last Friday." Mac tossed her backpack over her shoulder. "Maybe instead of whining about your practice routine you just need to man up."

"Man up?"

"Here we go again." Alyson grabbed Devon's arm and headed toward the car. "The way those two fight, you'd think they were brother and sister."

"Or something," Devon agreed. "You don't think there's some kind of romantic connection between them, do you?"

"Mac says they're just friends and I know she really cares about Eli, so I doubt it. I'm sure they've been friends so long they just have a brother/sister thing going on." Alyson would never say so to

Devon, but she was beginning to wonder how they really felt about each other herself. The feelings they shared were definitely complicated and intense.

Chapter 9

Alyson joined the others at their favorite table by the cafeteria window the next day. It was a sunny day that promised to provide unseasonably warm temperatures. It was barely noon, but the sea in the distance was already dotted with surfers waiting for the bigger waves that arrived most afternoons.

"So," Trevor began before Alyson could even be seated, "did you get a chance to work on the parchment last night?"

"I did."

"And?"

"And I have a partial translation. There were quite a few words I couldn't figure out, but from the ones I could translate, they seem to be written in the form of a riddle or code, just as we thought. To be honest, though, none of it really makes any sense." Alyson pulled a notepad out of her backpack and set in on the table next to her salad.

"Here's what I have so far. It seems like the directions start at 'Crisco's end.' Now, I don't know if Crisco is a person or maybe a river or trail or some other object. From 'the place of Crisco's end' a door appears when someone named Chuck sleeps."

"Okay, that's weird," Trevor admitted. "How are we ever going to figure out the directions to the treasure if we need to know who these people who have probably been dead for over a hundred and fifty years are?"

"It goes on to say that when the door appears, you ascend to a sacred gate. There are several words I haven't been able to translate yet, but then the word *right* appears. I don't know if it means you turn right or have to guess right, or maybe you must be righteous."

"I was really hoping once we translated this thing it would give us directions to the buried treasure in plain English," Eli whined. "How are we ever supposed to figure this out?"

"I don't know." Alyson looked up from her pad and took a sip of her diet soda. "Even if we manage to translate the rest of the words I'm not sure we can make any sense out of them."

"What else does it say?" Mac asked.

"After you either turn right or guess right or whatever, you must find the 'source of the mother's tears.'"

"Oh, great; this just keeps getting harder and harder." Trevor wadded up the wrapper from his cheeseburger. "Does it say whose mother? How are we supposed to figure out why some chick is crying if we don't even know who the chick is?"

"No, it doesn't indicate a specific mother. At least I don't think it does. I haven't translated all the words yet, so maybe there's a clue in the part of the parchment I haven't gotten to yet."

"Is there anything else?" Mac encouraged.

"There's something about heaven's window showing the way when the end of night turns into day. That's the only part that sort of makes sense."

"Sunrise of course," Devon contributed.

"I've seen movies where you have to be at a certain place at a certain time of day so the sunlight illuminates a spot on the ground or on a wall where a secret passage is," Trevor provided. "I'll bet it's something like that."

"It would make sense," Alyson agreed. "We just need to figure out the not-so-clear clues that come before this part so we know where we need to be at sunrise."

"Is there more?" Mac asked.

"This is my favorite part." Alyson groaned. "It says something about descending into endless darkness. It looks like it's in this endless darkness that we'll find the sacred ground."

"Our treasure," Eli guessed.

"Maybe; it doesn't actually say what will be found there. It does talk about the fact that those who are not blessed cannot enter." Alyson looked up at the group. "I don't know if that means you have to have received a certain blessing like a holy ritual, or you need to be blessed by the gods, as in having certain powers, or maybe you just need to be a good person or have good intent."

"Is that all?" Mac asked.

"It's all I could translate."

"So what's next?" Eli asked. "Where do we go from here?"

"Booker," Alyson and Mac said at the same time.

"Maybe he can help us figure out some more of this," Devon agreed. "Or maybe his journals have a reference to a Crisco or a Chuck."

"Trevor and I have practice," Eli reminded them, "but I'm dying to find out if you get any new information. Can we meet up somewhere after practice?"

"I'll call my mom," Alyson volunteered. "Maybe we can all get together at my house. I've been meaning to give you all the grand tour since the remodel on the first floor has been completed. It looks really great."

Alyson called her mom from her cell and she not only agreed to have everyone over after football practice but even said she'd make everyone dinner.

"My mouth is already watering." Trevor rubbed his hands together in anticipation. "Did she say what she was making?"

Alyson shook her head. "I guess it'll just have to be a surprise."

After school Devon met Alyson in the parking lot, then picked Mac up at Cybertech. Booker was waiting for them in the library when they arrived at his house. Coffee and scones were set out and a warm fire was crackling in the fireplace.

"You didn't have to go to all this trouble," Alyson greeted him.

"Nonsense. It was no trouble at all. I figured you might want a snack after a long day at school, and I did promise you some of Maggie's scones."

"Thank you. Everything looks delicious." Mac picked one up and took a bite.

"I translated some more of the parchment and wanted to see if you could help us make any sense out of it," Alyson began. "But first, why don't you tell us any new information you've uncovered."

"I did some more research on the *Santa Inez*. It seems something did happen to the captain while he was in port here. He came onshore but never returned to the ship. The crew wanted to organize a search for him, but the first mate made the decision to set sail the very next day. There's no indication why he decided on that course of action, but just days into the voyage he was found murdered in his cabin. Apparently, members of the crew began to blame one another not only for the first mate's death but also for the disappearance of the captain. Fighting broke out, which caused additional deaths as well as damage to the ship, forcing it to dock along the Baja coast."

"Did they ever find out who killed the first mate or what happened to the captain?" Devon asked.

"No, the reason for their demise remains a mystery to this day. Most of the ship's crew disbanded immediately upon docking and signed up with other ships. As far as I can tell, a thorough investigation was never conducted."

"Is there a list of the cargo that was taken from the ship anywhere?" Alyson asked.

"Actually, I did find such a list, but there was nothing on it that sounded anything like the statue."

"Maybe it was never on the ship," Mac suggested.

"Or maybe whoever had it snuck it off the ship when they docked," Devon guessed. "It could even have been lost at sea during the fighting."

"Was a ship's or captain's log one of the items listed?" Alyson asked. "It seems like in the movies the captain always keeps some sort of diary or log. Maybe we can find clues there."

Booker looked more closely at the list. "Not that I can see. It doesn't mean it wasn't found, however. Most of the things on here are items of value: cargo and weapons and such. There is one interesting note, though: a number of young native girls were on board."

"Why would they be on the ship?" Alyson asked. "Could they have been the sailors' girlfriends or something?"

"I believe they must have been slaves who were either to be traded or sold or possibly forced into prostitution for the crew's enjoyment. There are accounts in my research of local natives kidnapping young women from rival tribes and selling them into slavery or trading them to members of the ships' crews in exchange for things like tobacco and coffee."

"That's sick," Mac spat. "I thought the Chinook were a peaceful people."

"They were, but women were seen differently in those days. They were considered to be property, the same as any other object of value. During times of war or conflict any bounty that was recovered by the conquering tribe was considered currency."

"Okay," Devon began, "so far we have an old parchment with an encrypted message, a long-dead skeleton, probably the captain of the *Santa Inez*, a handful of gold coins, a missing sacred object, a dead first mate, and mutiny at sea."

"And a diary," Alyson added. "I've barely started the translation. There might be more to the puzzle in there."

"You said you'd managed to translate part of the parchment," Booker encouraged.

"Yes." Alyson pulled both the parchment and her partial translation out of her backpack and set it on the table. "It doesn't make much sense at this point, though."

Booker looked at Alyson's notes and considered the possible meaning of the encrypted message. "It seems obvious that end of night turning into day means sunrise."

"That's the only part we've been able to figure out," Devon confirmed. "That and the speculation that with the sunrise a spot on the floor or maybe a wall will be illuminated and reveal our next clue."

"The riddle starts off by talking about a couple of guys named Crisco and Chuck. How are we ever supposed to figure out what the writer means by that?" Mac asked.

"Yes, that could be a problem," Booker acknowledged. "The message was obviously directed toward a specific audience. The only reason I can even think of as to why the directions or message is in some kind of code in the first place is that the writer was protecting the information from someone who might have access to the document other than the intended audience."

"Any suggestions?" Mac asked.

"If you'll allow me to make a copy of your notes as well as the parchment, I'll work on this after supper to see if I can come up with anything. I have quite a few diaries and other original documents from that time period that I can use to search for references of someone by these names."

"Sure, no problem. In the meantime," Alyson added, "I'll work on translating the diary we found. Maybe we'll find a clue in there."

Devon, Mac, and Alyson let themselves out after promising to hook up with Booker the next day.

"Check out those guys weeding the flowerbeds." Mac pointed out two men in work clothes who seemed to be more interested in watching them than tending to their chores. "I thought Booker said the gardener came on Mondays and Fridays. Today is Wednesday."

"Maybe they're putting in a little overtime," Devon postulated.

"Maybe." Mac didn't seem convinced.

"Hi, Mom, we're home," Alyson called as she and the gang walked through the door an hour later.

"I'm in the kitchen," Sarah Prescott called back.

"Something smells wonderful." Trevor was drooling as he followed Alyson into the warm kitchen.

"You probably smell the apple pies I baked this afternoon."

"Apple is my favorite." Trevor walked over to the counter where the pies were cooling and took in a deep breath.

Dinner was delicious, as always: thick, creamy seafood alfredo served over fresh fettuccine noodles, hot crusty garlic bread, and a crisp green salad, followed by the pie topped with freshly whipped cream.

"How is your investigation into the missing relic coming along?" Mom asked as they all ate.

Alyson, Devon, and Mac filled everyone in on the conversation they'd had with Booker that afternoon.

"We're hoping the journal is in some way linked to the missing statue," Alyson explained. "There are so many missing pieces to the puzzle I'm not sure we're going to be able to figure this one out."

"I met your friend Booker at the museum yesterday. He's quite a character. A lot like his friend Charlie. He told me he'd been working with you on a school project. I put two and two together and figured out he must be helping out with your newest mystery."

"He's been a huge help," Alyson confirmed. "And you should see his house. It's huge, and filled to the brim with artwork and antiques. You'd love it. It's like visiting a museum. We're going by again after school tomorrow. You should come with us. I'm sure Booker wouldn't mind."

"I might do that if I can get away from the museum for a while. The opening is in a week and it seems like we still have so much to do. If I can't get away tomorrow maybe some other time."

The dinner conversation gravitated toward the huge success of the football team this season, the state championships, and school in general. By the time the final bite of the delicious pie had been eaten everyone was feeling the pressure of neglected homework and impending deadlines.

"I really should get home." Mac set her napkin on her empty plate. "I've been so busy researching the town's history that I've completely ignored the history paper I have due for Mr. Evans at the end of the week."

"Tell me about it," Alyson said. "I haven't even started mine. Translating the journal may have to wait for another time. It'd be kind of ironic to flunk history because you're so busy researching history."

"We have that English paper coming up too," Mac reminded her. "Maybe we should see if Booker has time to work on the journal. We could bring him all the stuff you've done so far."

"That's a good idea." Alyson got up from the table and started clearing dishes. "I'll call him later to see if he's willing to work it. We can drop everything off when we go by there tomorrow afternoon."

Chapter 10

Alyson, Devon, and Mac visited Booker the next day as planned. The elderly man had agreed to work on translating the journal, so Alyson had brought everything she'd accumulated that she thought might help him with his task. Alyson's mom had confirmed that, as expected, she was too busy to join them that afternoon, but Booker had stopped by the museum earlier, and when she'd expressed a desire to see his house he had told her he would be honored to give her a private tour at any time.

"Seems like Booker might be a bit of a flirt," Mac observed as Alyson filled her in.

"Yeah, I kind of picked up on that the first time I met him."

"I wonder why he isn't married," Mac mused. "He's obviously rich and he seems smart and witty. You'd think someone would have snapped him up a long time ago."

"Maybe he was married. Before, I mean. He could be divorced or a widower. Of course he could also just be a confirmed bachelor. There are people who are so set in their ways that they don't play well with others."

Booker greeted them at the front door and led them to the library. It seemed that afternoons with Booker were becoming a regular thing.

"That's odd," Booker said.

He had books, sheets of yellowed documents, notepads, and handwritten journals spread out on every available surface in the room.

"What's odd?" Alyson asked.

"I could swear I left the parchment here with the other things."

Alyson was looking at Mac as Maggie came into the room holding the parchment. "You left this in your office. I thought you might need it."

"Thanks, Maggie. I must be losing my mind." Booker was fluttering around, clearing space on the sofas for his visitors. "Help yourself to some coffee or a sandwich. I've been busy researching our little mystery ever since you left yesterday. I think I've uncovered some information that might help us decipher the map. I've been so anxious to share the information I've uncovered with you that I could hardly contain myself until you got here."

Maggie left the room, closing the door behind her.

Alyson, Mac, and Devon each poured cups of coffee and sat down on the sofa Booker had cleared.

"It definitely looks like you've been busy," Alyson said.

"Yes indeed. I hadn't realized how many original documents I had pertaining to this particular time period until I started researching. I haven't been this excited about anything in years. I'm so glad you decided to let me be a part of your little adventure."

"You said you had some new information regarding the parchment," Devon said, getting right to the point.

"I found out that Crisco was the name of a ship that sank during the early part of the nineteenth century," Booker jumped right in.

"So starting the journey at the place of *Crisco*'s end would mean the spot where the ship went down," Devon concluded.

"It would seem so."

"But do we know where the site of the shipwreck is?" Alyson asked.

"We do indeed." Booker enthusiastically sifted through a pile of yellowed charts and graphs on the table in front of him. "I've gone back and read all the accounts I could find of the actual event. As far as I can tell, the ship sank in Cutter's Cove, not all that far from where the Cutter house now stands."

"So somewhere in the bay near my house," Alyson concluded.

"Exactly. Just off the point. I don't know whether the ship is still out there. Sunken ships tend to shift with the tide. But I believe our writer wasn't so much concerned with the actual location of the sunken ship as the point of its original demise."

"So the message should read that a door would appear near the spot where the *Crisco* sank when Chuck sleeps," Devon said.

"That still doesn't make any sense," Mac pointed out. "Does it mean the door appears at night?"

"Actually, it took a while, but I've discovered that the Chinook jargon word for water is *chuck*. If we place the word *water* into the riddle we have a door appearing when water sleeps."

"When water sleeps?" Devon asked. "What does that mean?"

"I've never really known water to sleep," Alyson agreed.

"No, but maybe the writer meant when water is at its calmest," Mac suggested. "Or its lowest point. Like low tide."

"That would make sense." Devon nodded. "The entrance to a cave system could very well be revealed at low tide. The doorway may be underwater the rest of the time."

"So we just need to go to the spot where the *Crisco* sank at low tide and find the doorway that leads to the clues in the rest of the message," Mac enthused.

"Yeah, but what if the doorway is the only way in or out and the tide has risen by the time we want to get out?" Alyson asked.

"Good point," Mac acknowledged. "I guess this whole thing might be sort of risky."

"We'd really better think this thing through," Devon agreed. "We should be sure we have all the supplies we need before we try entering the cave system. Ropes, flashlights, batteries, food and water, and warm clothing. It's possible we won't be able to get out until the next low tide."

"What if the cave fills with water when the tide comes in?" Alyson asked. "Maybe we should bring scuba gear."

"The message says that once the door appears you ascend to the sacred gate," Booker reminded them. "My guess is that the clues provided will lead to a journey that begins at sea level and then ascends into the caves up on the bluffs."

"Like the one near my house," Alyson said. "If the *Crisco* sank near the end of the point near my house it makes sense that the cave we found is part of that system. The room where we found the body and the box might even be the sacred gate itself. There were two tunnels leading from the room. One might go down to the ocean floor and the other might be the gateway to the rest of the message."

"Maybe we should start off in the cave near your house and see if one of the tunnels leads us to a sea-level entrance near the point," Devon suggested. "We could go at low tide to see if a doorway exists."

"Yeah, but which tunnel do we take?" Mac asked.

"The tunnel should descend toward the ocean floor, so we can probably figure out if we're in the correct one by the degree and direction of the incline," Devon said.

"The next clue in the message is the one in which Alyson translated the word *right*," Booker joined in. "She wasn't sure if it meant to turn right or guess right or even be righteous. I've been working on translating the words surrounding the word *right*, and I believe the message directs the reader to take the right-hand tunnel. The word *kloshe*, which translates to right, is followed by the word *lemah*, which means hand." Booker spread the parchment out on the table in front of them. "The word *wayhut*," he pointed to it, "seems to translate to path or trail."

"So, the journey continues down the right-hand tunnel, which means we should follow the left-hand tunnel to the sea," Mac concluded. "Does anyone know what time low tide is?"

"I've taken the liberty of checking the tide tables for the next few weeks," Booker offered.

"So you knew what sleeping water referred to before we even got here," Alyson said. "Why didn't you just tell us rather than having us work it out?"

"It's no fun to bc given all the answers to a riddle," Booker answered. "Half of the fun in solving a mystery is the process of discovery. Besides, you all figured it out a lot faster than I did. It actually took me several hours before the light in my brain went on."

"I've found it helps to have multiple brains working on a problem. I would never have figured out the mystery of the missing heir if I hadn't had Mac, Devon, Trevor, and Eli helping me."

"And if you hadn't figured that out, the town might not be getting the wonderful museum that's about to open," Booker added. "I went by this morning and spoke to your beautiful mother. She's quite the looker, let me tell you. If I were thirty years younger... Anyway, she informed me that she was interested in taking a tour of my home. I'd be honored to entertain her at any time."

"I'm sure she'd love that. She's an artist, so she has a great appreciation of art and antiques. And the architecture of this place is truly spectacular."

"Why, thank you. I'm very proud of it. I took a colonial approach but added a few of my own style twists."

"Low tide is at 8:59 a.m. tomorrow and 9:59 a.m. Saturday," Devon interrupted. "When do you propose we check out the left-hand tunnel to see if we're on track with the rest of the riddle?"

"Well, tomorrow is the big game," Mac reminded them. "We can't miss that."

"I've heard how splendidly our local football team has done this year," Booker said. "I've always loved a good game. Perhaps I'll attend myself. Will your lovely mother be there?"

"I'm sure she will."

"Well, perhaps I'll see her there. We can arrange a time for her visit."

"I'm not busy this weekend." Devon again brought the subject back to the reason they were there. "Perhaps we should try to get together on Saturday. If low tide's at 9:59 we should probably meet at Alyson's by 7:30 or so. If our hypothesis is correct about the location of the doorway and the path to it, I doubt it will take more than an hour to hike down to the entrance, but we should allow more time just in case. If we can enter the tunnel by 8:00 it will give us two hours."

"Seven thirty on a Saturday. Not really my cup of tea, especially after the big victory party I'm sure will take place tomorrow night. But I'm in," Mac said,

"Me too," Alyson agreed.

"We'll check with Eli and Trevor this evening," Devon confirmed. "How about you, Booker? Want to come along?"

"You have no idea how much I'd like to, but I'm afraid my old bones wouldn't be up to the task. I'd love it if one of you would call me with the results of your journey, though, no matter what time you get back. I'm sure I'll be on pins and needles all day. In the meantime, I'll content myself with working on the journal. By the way, Alyson, I did a bit of research about a possible curse associated with the statue."

"And . . . ?"

"And I found a notation in one of my books. It's quite interesting, really. It states that anyone who tries to touch the statue and is not pure of heart will come to a painful end, doomed to walk in the periphery between life and death, never to find peace or completion."

"Like a ghost?"

"Yes, I guess so."

"Wow, did you hear what Booker said about the curse?" Mac asked as they got into the car. "Do you think your nocturnal visitor has been affected by the curse and now is in some kind of limbo between life and death?"

"Maybe. He really wanted me to find that parchment. Maybe if we find the statue and return it to its rightful place the curse will be lifted."

"I hope so." Mac checked the time. "The guys should be finishing up with practice right about now. Let's swing by the school to check with them about Saturday. That doesn't leave us much time to get our supplies together. We probably should come up with a plan today as to who's going to be responsible for bringing what."

Trevor and Eli were as enthusiastic about the plans for Saturday as the other three. They all agreed that Devon and Eli would be responsible for ropes and climbing equipment; they already had most of it anyway. Mac offered to stock up on batteries and everyone would be responsible for their own flashlights and warm clothes. Alyson volunteered to bring along snacks and water bottles. Everyone agreed to meet at Alyson's at seven thirty on Saturday morning, where she promised to have plenty of coffee and hot muffins waiting for them.

Chapter 11

Friday morning dawned bright and sunny, a perfect day for football and the huge rally that was set to precede the game. Alyson dressed in her favorite pair of jeans, her royal blue and gray Seacliff Pirates sweatshirt, and new Nike tennis shoes. She pulled her long blond hair into a ponytail and tied one blue and one gray ribbon around the hair band. She applied a minimal amount of makeup to complement her casual attire but later added a wisp of blue eye shadow. By the time the game was over it would probably be freezing cold, so she grabbed her blue goose down jacket and put blue cashmere gloves in her shoulder bag.

"You look like you've got school spirit," her mom greeted her as she bounded down the stairs and into the kitchen for breakfast.

"I do, don't I? Can you ever in a million years envision Amanda wearing something like this no matter what the occasion?"

"Not really. The way you talk about her in the third person makes it seem as if she's a totally different person. I mean, you are her and she is you. If it's within you to demonstrate school spirit it must have been somewhere within her too."

"I know it seems weird, but I really feel like a different person. Amanda would never fit into my life now, any more than the person I've become would have fit into my life in New York. Amanda would have died before she attended school in a sweatshirt and tennis shoes.

"I guess a lot really has changed in the past few months," her mom acknowledged. "Do you ever miss it? Your old life?"

"Not really. I thought I would, but I love living here. There's an energy and depth now that my life in New York never had. I do on occasion miss the shopping, though. I was hoping you would take Mac and me to San Francisco for the post-holiday sales during winter break."

"Sounds like fun. I could do with a little shopping spree myself."

"Go, Pirates," Mac greeted her as she joined her in first period. Mac was dressed in a matching Pirates sweatshirt and faded jeans, but she'd gone to the extra step of wearing her hair in pigtails, one dyed blue and the other gray.

"I hope that hair color is temporary." Alyson settled herself onto the stool next to her.

"Yeah, it'll wash right out."

"I love the blue lipstick. It matches perfectly with your blue nail polish," Alyson teased.

"Hey, I notice a hint of blue eye shadow on your own eyelids."

"Yeah, I'm fully immersed in the whole school spirit thing. Go, Pirates." Alyson shot her fist in the air.

"Hey, guys," Chelsea greeted the pair as she took her seat behind them. "Are you both ready to cheer tonight until you can cheer no more?"

"I've been warming up my tonsils all morning," Alyson confirmed. "Aren't you freezing in that cheerleading outfit? They should make cheerleading pants for such cold days."

"My legs do get a little cold, but I figure if the guys can play in subfreezing weather I can cheer in it. I've got nylons on, and they help a little. Have you seen Trevor this morning?"

"I talked to him last night," Mac said. "He said the whole team was skipping classes this morning so they could get in the zone before the game. They're all meeting in the gym to go over plays and stuff. We get out of school early for the rally anyway, so all the teachers agreed not to hold their absences against them."

"Hey, how come the cheerleaders don't get out of class? This game is as big a deal for us as it is for them," Chelsea complained.

"I don't know; you'll have to ask your coach. Maybe she didn't see the need for her cheerleaders to spend the morning zoning."

"It's not fair. The football players are getting all the special privileges and glory that go along with having a winning season. What people don't take into account is that they never would have gotten this far if we hadn't been there to cheer them on. What we do is an integral part of the whole process."

"I feel your pain," Alyson sympathized. "Go, cheerleaders."

Chelsea raised her hand as Mr. Harris walked into the room.

"Yes, Miss Green?"

"Can I be excused from class on account of the rally and all?"

"I wasn't aware the cheerleaders were meeting."

"It's sort of a last-minute thing."

"I wasn't planning on doing much today anyway because we have a shortened period, so I guess it's okay, but bring me a note from your coach on Monday."

"Sure, Mr. Harris." Chelsea began gathering up her things. "I'll see you at the rally."

"What is she going to do?" Mac whispered to Alyson. "It's not like the cheerleaders really are meeting or anything. Is she just going to go sit somewhere by herself?"

"If I know Chelsea, she'll probably go around and find the other cheerleaders and get them all out of class too. She doesn't seem like the type who likes to be bested."

"For those of us who don't have football-related activities, please open your books to chapter twelve," Mr. Harris said from the front of the room.

The rest of the day went by quickly. Alyson and Mac went to their usual table for lunch.

"Are Trevor and Eli doing the team thing for lunch too?" Alyson asked Devon, who sat there alone.

"Appears so."

Alyson sat down next to Devon and gave him a quick kiss on the lips.

"I was planning to go to the sporting and climbing store to get some extra supplies for tomorrow after the rally. Do you want to come?" Devon asked.

"Sure. How about you, Mac?" Alyson asked.

"No thanks. I didn't get quite as caught up with my work as you did. My sisters were rehearsing their lines for the Thanksgiving play all night and it was hard to concentrate. I think I'll go to the library after the rally."

"I'd love to come to the play. When is it?" Alyson asked.

"It's Tuesday at seven in the elementary school cafeteria."

"Want to go, Dev? Maybe we could do dinner before."

"Sounds good. I'll pick you up at five thirty."

"I kind of wanted to get to the rally early," Mac interrupted. "I want to get a good seat near the front, so I can cheer Eli and Trevor on."

"Sure," Alyson agreed. "I'll finish up my sandwich and then we can head over to the gym."

The rally was both loud and spirited. Alyson had to hand it to Chelsea and the other cheerleaders; they did a good job, their routines well-choreographed and -executed. Alyson found herself really getting into the spirit of the occasion. Chelsea might be just a little off about the fact that the team couldn't have had such a great season without the cheerleaders, but she could see they worked as hard on their sport as the guys did on theirs.

"That was really fun," Alyson told Devon as they walked to his Expedition after the rally.

"Yeah. I especially like that dance number the cheerleaders did at the end."

"Chelsea is always going on and on about how hard they work, and I have to admit their show really did make it look like they'd put hours and hours of rehearsal into it."

Alyson looked out the window at the coastline as they drove toward the next town, which had a sporting superstore that carried every type of outdoor gear imaginable.

"Guess everyone is stocking up on camping supplies. The place is packed," Devon commented. "I hope we can find a parking spot."

"It looks like someone's pulling out just ahead," Alyson pointed out.

Devon parked and they walked the short distance to the entrance.

"Wow, this place is great." Alyson looked around at the floor-to-ceiling sporting equipment. The store seemed to have equipment to meet the needs of every type of sporting enthusiast, from scuba divers to baseball players to hunters and hockey players.

"Let's start in the climbing department and work our way to the front," he suggested.

They made their way to the back of the store and started gathering the supplies they would need. "Maybe we should get some of these hard hats with lights attached," Alyson suggested. "They'd free up our hands for climbing or carrying stuff."

"Good idea. Grab five."

"I only see two."

"I'll ask at the front if they have more in stock."

"Sorry," the man behind the counter said when Devon tracked him down. "I haven't sold any since I've worked here and not ten minutes ago I sold the other three I had in the back. I can special order some if you want."

"Thanks, I'll let you know."

"Wow, that's a coincidence," Alyson commented. She looked around as Devon checked out. There were two men three checkstands over who looked familiar, but she couldn't quite place them. They seemed to be embroiled in an intense conversation.

"See those two guys arguing over at checkstand four?" Alyson whispered. "Do you recognize them?"

Devon studied the pair for a minute. "No, I can't say that I do."

"I have the feeling I've seen them somewhere before."

"A lot of people from Cutter's Cove shop here. Maybe you've seen them in town."

"Maybe."

One of the men looked up and stared directly at Alyson. She gasped. Suddenly she knew exactly where she had seen them before.

"What is it?" Devon asked.

"I'll tell you in the car. Let's get out of here."

Alyson filled Devon in on the men she'd seen in Booker's garden the other day. "I'm sure they were the same guys."

"So?"

"What do you mean, so? Don't you think it's suspicious?"

"Not really. You saw two gardeners at the home of a man who has a huge garden. Then two days later they show up at a large sporting goods store where lots of people shop. I'd say it's a coincidence."

"There sure are a lot of coincidences cropping up lately."

"You need to relax. I think you're seeing conspiracies where none exist."

The game was a close one, but in the end the Seacliff Pirates were victorious, and for the first time in the team's history they were going to the state championship. The noise level at the Cannery when the gang arrived was deafening, and there was not only nowhere to sit but nowhere to stand.

"I've never seen this place so packed," Mac yelled over the noise.

"Yeah, and I'm starving," Trevor said. "There's no way we're getting a table any time soon."

"We could go eat somewhere else, then come back later when things have calmed down a bit," Alyson suggested.

"Sounds fine to me," Eli agreed. "We should probably go say hi to the coach first, though."

"You guys go get the car while Eli and I make the rounds," Trevor said. "We'll meet you out in front in a couple of minutes."

Alyson, Mac, and Devon headed out to the parking lot. They decided to drive around to the front of the building so Trevor and Eli could just hop in when they came out. When they appeared Trevor had Chelsea in tow.

"Oh, great," Mac complained. "Look who's with Trev."

"Come on, Mac," Alyson whispered. "She's okay. She's probably hungry too. You have to admit the cheerleaders really do expend almost as much energy as the team."

"Where to?" Devon asked after everyone had piled in and taken their seats.

"How about the café downtown?" Trevor suggested. "I could go for a huge steak and some fries."

The café was crowded too with the after-game crowd, but they managed to get a table for six in the back.

"It looks like the Pirates' victory is good for business for everyone," Mac observed. "Even the drive-in hamburger joint down the street was packed when we drove by."

"Well, I for one am starving." Trevor buttered a roll from the bread basket the waitress had set on the table and shoved the whole thing in his mouth.

"Me too." Chelsea opened her menu to peruse the options. "I swear, I've never cheered so hard in my life. When the other team pulled ahead toward the end of the fourth quarter I thought I'd die. But, as usual, the dynamite team of Johnson and Stevenson pulled it out in the end."

"Yeah, you guys were great." Mac hugged Eli's arm. "Although these close games are seriously taking a few years off my life. I don't know how I'll make it through the state championships."

"When are they anyway?" Alyson asked.

"In two weeks," Eli answered. "It's going to be tough. There will be some really good teams with a lot more experience than we have, but it should be fun."

"Are you ready to order?" a harried-looking waitress asked.

"I'll have the sixteen-ounce steak, medium rare, with fries and a salad," Trevor began.

"I'll have the same," Eli said.

"I'll have an eight-ounce fillet, medium, with steamed rice and a salad." Chelsea closed her menu and looked toward the others.

"I'll just have a seafood salad with dressing on the side," Alyson ordered.

"Ditto for me. I don't think I've quite digested the hot dog and fries I had at the game quite yet," Mac added.

"And you, sir?" The waitress looked toward Devon, who was still reading his menu.

"I'll just have a meatloaf sandwich."

Alyson held up the glass of water the waitress had just brought. "I propose a toast. To Trevor and Eli and the rest of the Seacliff High Pirates for an excellent game and an excellent season."

Chelsea cleared her throat.

"And to the cheerleaders, who supported them all the way," Alyson added.

"Hear, hear." Everyone clinked glasses.

"So do you guys have practice tomorrow?" Chelsea asked. "I mean, state is only two weeks away."

"Coach gave us the whole weekend off," Trevor told her. "Which means we should be able to go ahead with our plans for tomorrow without a conflict."

"What plans?" Chelsea asked.

"Just more research stuff," Mac answered quickly.

"I swear, you people have the most boring lives. All you do is hang out in libraries. You really ought to try to get out more."

"Yeah, boring." Mac smiled.

Chapter 12

The guys arrived bright and early the next morning. Devon gave Alyson a casual kiss hello and asked her if she'd remembered to pack a leash for Tucker. Alyson filled her mom in on exactly what their plans were, where they planned to go, and when they thought they'd be back. If anything went wrong someone would know where to look.

"Okay, we each need to be sure we have a flashlight, and we should bring something to mark our way in case the tunnel forks off," Devon instructed. "The last thing we want to do is get lost in there."

"There's some spray paint out in the shed," Alyson said. "And there are some extra flashlights in there too. I have some snacks and bottled water we can carry with us."

"I've got the ropes and other climbing equipment we might need," Eli added.

"And I've got batteries." Mac held up a supersize pack.

"Okay, is everyone ready?" Devon asked as they neared the opening of the cave. "Be sure to stay together, to watch where you're walking, and to be aware of what's overhead. We don't want anyone getting hurt. I'll go first, then the girls, and Eli and Trevor will bring up the rear. If we get to any junctions we'll mark our path with the spray paint."

Devon started his descent into the underground room, followed by Alyson and Tucker, and then Mac, Eli, and finally Trevor.

The room was large and tall enough for them to walk upright. "It's so dark in here," Mac commented, "even with the flashlights. I can't imagine being in here without any light. It would be horrifying."

Mac shone her flashlight toward the far corner where their friend, the skeleton, still waited. "Maybe we'll actually be able to figure out what happened to him. When this is all over maybe we should give him a proper burial or something."

"We'll take the tunnel to the left, as originally planned," Devon instructed. "The parchment didn't mention any forks in the road between here and the ocean floor, if this even is the room that was referred to in it, but if we do come across any, Trevor will mark the fork we take with the paint."

They started through the left-hand tunnel, walking slowly and shining their flashlights all around them. The tunnel was a good four feet wide and eight feet high. The walls were uneven yet worn smooth by some natural force, which could have occurred thousands, even millions of years before. As the tunnel wound its way deeper into the interior it began to descend, gradually at first, then more and more steeply.

"I feel like we're climbing down the side of a mountain." Mac placed her hands against the side wall of the cavern for extra support. "It's really steep. You do realize we're going to have to come back up this way? I'm not sure my poor legs can take it. How far do you think we've gone?"

Devon stopped and checked something he held in his hand.

"About a quarter of a mile. If we keep descending at this rate it shouldn't be long now."

They continued to walk for several more minutes before things began to level out and widen.

"We must be at sea level now," Trevor said, "or close to it. I can hear waves crashing nearby."

Devon stopped. "I can see an opening in the tunnel in the distance, but the water is still coming in. We're here a little early. I don't think we can go much farther until the tide goes down the rest of the way."

"It's sort of strange and scary to think that the very place we're standing was underwater just a few minutes ago." Mac touched the still damp wall next to her. "I hope we're right about the whole low-tide thing and some big wave doesn't come crashing through and drown us."

"That's why I think we should hang back until the tide is all the way out and the tunnel is completely in the clear." Devon turned around and looked at Alyson, who had been quiet during the trip through the tunnel. "Are you okay?"

"Yeah, I'm fine." She smiled at him. "I was just thinking about phantom waves and how screwed we'd be if one of those happened along. It's sort of claustrophobic in here."

Devon put his arm around her shoulders and squeezed. Tucker whimpered as a large wave crashed through the opening, sending thunderous echoes through the tunnel.

"Maybe we should retreat a little farther back until low tide actually arrives." Devon looked at his watch. "It shouldn't be long."

"What's that?" Mac pointed to something in the distance.

"It looks like a small boat." Devon squinted, trying to see out the cave opening and into the open sea. "It's pretty far away, but I think I see two, maybe three people on board. Probably fishermen."

"Or someone looking for our cave opening," Mac suggested. "We've kind of already verified that the tunnel goes down to the ocean floor and that the entrance is underwater for much of the day. Is it really necessary to wait for low tide?"

"Mac has a point," Alyson agreed. "It seems like we have enough to go on to head back to the room where we entered and take the right-hand tunnel. If we're correct in our assumptions we should come across something resembling mother's tears, whatever that means."

"Makes sense to me," Eli agreed. "I say we head back now rather than waiting. If Mac is right and the men in the boat are coming here, we don't want them to see us. It might arouse their curiosity. The climb back to the first room is going to take a lot longer than the trip down."

"I'm in," Trevor agreed.

"Okay, I'll take the lead again," Devon said. "The climb is going to be steep; if anyone needs to stop to rest just say so."

The climb down had taken under an hour, the climb back up almost two. By the time they left the tunnel and got back into the room where they'd started everyone was exhausted.

"If this is indeed the gate referred to on the parchment I wonder why the writer called it that," Mac said. "I mean, there's no gate, real or symbolic, that I can see."

Eli shrugged. "Maybe there used to be some sort of gate. I mean, the parchment was written almost two hundred years ago."

"Yeah, I guess," Mac acknowledged. "Which brings me to my next question. If the gate room no longer has a gate, what if the other clues are no longer valid? Eli's right; a lot can change in two hundred years."

Alyson stopped momentarily. "How long do we look for the next clue, mother's tears? I mean, we could walk around for days and never come across anything resembling mother's tears if it no longer exists. Booker said there are miles and miles of caverns in this area."

"If we assume the trip was to take place in a single day we can probably make some assumptions about how long the journey should take," Devon pointed out.

"Uh, guys, I just had another thought," Mac said. "If the journey is supposed to take place in a single day then how would the traveler get out? If you can only access the tunnel during low tide the traveler would have to wait until the following low tide to get out."

"That's true," Trevor agreed. "I think we have to assume the total trip would take around twelve hours. Besides that, the traveler would have to wait for sunrise to solve that specific part of the riddle. If low tide was early—say one or two in the morning—the traveler could conceivably make it to heaven's window by sunrise, then back to the cave entrance by the next low tide."

"Yeah, but we've missed sunrise today and I'm not real keen on spending the night in this dark, cold cave," Alyson spoke up. "Besides, I told my mom I'd be back by around five or six."

"Okay, here's the plan." Devon shone his flashlight on the directions he was holding. "We'll try to make it to the point where the sunrise is supposed to reveal the next clue, then come back tomorrow at sunrise and proceed from there. We don't need to wait for low tide because we can climb out through the opening near Alyson's house."

"How will we know we're at heavens window?" Trevor asked. "Maybe it only reveals itself at sunrise."

Devon looked at his watch. "It's almost twelve thirty now. I say we search the caves until three o'clock, then head back whether we've found anything or not. We can always try again another day when we can get an earlier start if we need to."

They continued to walk in silence for several minutes. The walls seemed to be getting narrower as they wound their way deeper and deeper into the tunnel.

"It looks like we have our first fork in the road." Devon stopped walking and turned to face the others behind him.

"What fork?" Eli asked. "The parchment didn't say anything about a fork."

"Actually," Alyson pointed out, "we only managed to translate about half the words. A fork could very well have been mentioned in one of the sections we were unable to translate."

"So what do we do now?" Mac leaned against the wall behind her.

"I guess we just pick a direction and check it out," Alyson answered. "Question is, which way do we try first?"

Devon turned toward Alyson. "Pick one."

"I don't know. Right, I guess," she said.

"Be sure to mark our passage with the paint," Devon reminded Trevor. "We wouldn't want to get lost in here."

The walls were much closer together than they had been, and they had to suck in their breath and squeeze through at points. The farther they traveled the tighter the passage became.

"This is really claustrophobic," Mac commented as she scooted along with her back to one wall and her nose to the other.

"I think we should just go back the way we came in," Eli suggested.

"I don't think Tucker is liking this much." Alyson couldn't really see the dog—he was walking directly in front of her and she couldn't move her head—but she could hear him starting to whimper.

"We can't go much farther anyway," Devon added. "It looks like the tunnel dead-ends a few yards up."

They slowly inched their way back along the narrow passage in reverse. When they got back to the junction Devon looked at his watch. "It's almost two o'clock; we only have about an hour before we need to go back. Should we try the other tunnel or go back now?"

"I say we keep going," Trevor voiced his opinion from the rear.

"Okay, we keep looking." Devon started walking down the left-hand tunnel as the others followed. "At least this tunnel is roomier than the last one."

"Yeah, but it's really steep," Mac complained.

"We're probably climbing up the inside of one of the cliff faces that run along the coast," Trevor hypothesized. "You'd think the volcano or whatever created these caverns could have created switchbacks too. This really is quite a climb."

"I'll bet we come out on top of Smuggler's Bluff," Eli guessed. "I've been at the top and looked down to the ocean below and it's quite a ways down."

"Do you think we've gone that far?" Alyson asked. "I know we've been walking for hours, but we didn't exactly take the direct route. Smuggler's Bluff is a good mile or two from where we started."

"But none of the hills directly surrounding your house seem like they're high enough to create this steep a climb," Eli said. "I guess we'll just have to see where this tunnel finally ends up."

Devon stopped walking. "I'm afraid it ends right here."

"What?" Alyson squeezed in beside him and pointed her flashlight ahead of her. "I see lots more tunnel up ahead."

"Look down."

"Oh."

"What is it?" Mac asked from behind them.

Alyson pointed her flashlight down toward her feet. "Take Tucker back there with you," she said, nudging the dog behind her. "The trail just ends. There's a straight drop-off that's so deep I can't see the bottom."

"It's a good thing you were watching where you were going," Trevor said to Devon.

"Tell me about it."

"Can we get across?" Eli asked.

Devon squinted into the darkness. "The break in the trail is at least ten feet. I can see where it picks up on the other side but no way to bridge the gap. Something must have caused this part of the cavern floor to erode."

"It sounds like the ocean below," Alyson observed. "Maybe the ocean comes in through some underground system during high tide and after years of erosion this part of the cavern fell into the sea."

Everyone stood quietly, listening to the sound of crashing waves coming from somewhere down below. Tucker barked once, probably in displeasure that he had been relocated from Alyson's side.

"Listen to the way sound echoes in here." Mac reached down to scratch Tucker behind the ears in an offer of comfort.

"So what now?" Trevor asked.

Devon continued to study the situation. "There's a narrow ledge along the far wall. I think I can make it across with the help of the climbing gear we brought. Once I get to the other side maybe I could rig up something the rest of you could use to get across."

"Sounds dangerous," Alyson cautioned.

"Not really; Eli and I go climbing with our dad all the time. I think we brought everything we need."

Devon checked his gear, then started slowly along the narrow lip that lined the cavern wall. Eli took the lead position of those waiting behind and fed Devon rope as needed. Every few feet he pounded a spike into the wall and wound the rope around it.

Alyson held her breath as Devon continued to work his way to the other side of the chasm. He seemed to know what he was doing, but she couldn't stand the tension of waiting. After what seemed like hours, he finally made his way to the other side.

"It's actually not too bad," Devon called. "The ledge is wider than it looks, and with the added security of the rope to hold on to, I think you should all make it fine."

"You think we should all go across?" Mac groaned.

"What about Tucker?" Alyson asked. "Do you think he can make it?"

"I'll come back across and we'll devise a harness to support him in case he slips. Dogs are pretty agile, but if he does stumble the harness will catch him and we'll pulley him across."

"Oh, he'd love that." Alyson shuddered. She knelt down to wrap her arms around Tucker, who licked the side of her face.

Devon worked his way across the chasm much quicker this time, now that he had the rope railing to hang on to for support. He spread out the remaining climbing supplies on the cavern floor and, with Eli and Trevor's help, fashioned a harness for Tucker.

"It's not fancy," Devon said after securing the makeshift harness under Tucker's belly and across his chest, "but it should hold. We'll tie a rope to each end and Eli will keep the rope taut as Tucker makes his way across the ledge. If he slips, I'll pull him over from the other side while Eli adjusts the tension on this one."

"Do you think he'll go?" Mac asked.

"I'll go across with Alyson," Devon instructed. "You hold on to Tucker's leash until we get across, then Alyson will call for him and you let him go."

Alyson hugged Tucker tighter, causing him to whimper. "It's okay, boy. Don't be scared. Everything will be fine."

"Come on." Devon took Alyson by the hand and led her across the chasm with the help of the security rope.

When they got to the other side Devon and Eli adjusted the tension of the rope through Tucker's harness and instructed Mac to take off his leash. As soon as the leash was unhooked, Tucker scampered across the ledge and into Alyson's waiting arms without any trouble at all. Devon untied the rope and removed the harness.

"Okay, Mac, you're next. Just take it slow," Devon said.

Mac was halfway across when her right shoe slipped once, causing dirt and rocks to plummet to the ocean below. She instinctively let go of the rope to catch herself.

"No, Mac, hold on."

Alyson screamed, her voice echoing through the caverns.

Chapter 13

Eli, who was right behind her, grabbed her arm and held on tight. "I've got you. Stand up slowly and grab the rope."

Mac slowly stood upright, grabbed the rope, and continued across. "I so don't want to do that again."

"We'll have to go back across on the way back unless we find another way out," Eli pointed out. "Don't worry; I won't let you fall. We could use Tucker's harness to help support you if you want."

"I'll be okay. That near slip just freaked me out, that's all. I'm not turning down the harness idea at this point, though."

They took a short break to regroup and store away the climbing equipment, then continued on their way through the dark cavern.

"We must be getting short on time," Mac said. "Getting across the chasm alone must have taken almost an hour."

Devon stopped to look at his watch. "Almost. What do you want to do? Keep going or head back?"

"Let's keep going for a little while," Alyson suggested. "We went to all the trouble of getting across the chasm; we might as well see what's on the other side."

"Yeah," Trevor agreed, "let's try to at least find the first clue—mother's tears."

They walked in silence, each lost in thought, for another twenty minutes before coming to another crossroads.

"So do we stay to the left or head to the right?" Devon asked once again.

Mac listened carefully. "I hear water. It sounds like a waterfall."

"I hear it too," Alyson said. "The sound is really faint, but I think it's coming from the tunnel on the right."

"Might be mother's tears," Trevor pointed out. "I vote we go that way."

They continued on for another fifteen minutes as the sound of water falling got louder and louder.

"You've got to see this," Devon exclaimed as the narrow tunnel gave way to a small room. At the end was a pool of water approximately fifteen feet in diameter, a shower of water falling a good twenty-five feet into it from someplace overhead.

"There must be a stream or spring on the surface that's feeding this," Trevor surmised.

"Yeah, but where does the water go?" Eli asked. "It seems like with that amount of water streaming in here on a steady basis the pool would overflow and flood the cave."

"It must empty into some kind of underground stream somewhere below the pool's surface," Mac guessed. "The amount of water going out must be fairly equal to the amount coming in, thereby keeping the water level in the pool fairly consistent."

"I wonder where the stream empties out." Alyson walked over to the pool and tried to peer into its depths. The water was clear but dark; to the naked eye it appeared bottomless.

"Probably the ocean," Mac answered.

Alyson knelt down on one knee and touched the dark liquid. She could see her hand below the surface of the clear liquid. "Do you think there's life in here? You know, fish and stuff."

"I don't know." Mac shrugged. "It's possible, I suppose. The water seems pure enough, but it's almost completely dark in here. Most forms of life require at least some light to survive."

"But why mother's tears?" Trevor asked. "If this is the clue, why not just say water falling or something?"

Alyson pointed her flashlight overhead toward the source of the waterfall.

"It looks like the water is simply falling through the wall. Maybe there's something on the surface that looks like a mother. Or maybe I translated the parchment wrong. Or maybe we're in the wrong place altogether."

"That's a lot of maybes." Mac sighed. "Besides, if this is the right place, there should be another clue as to where to go next. Does anyone see a clue?"

Everyone looked around. The room was completely empty except for the waterfall and the pool below. There was no tunnel leading into or away from the room other than the one they had come in from. There was no writing on the walls or any evidence of anything else that might serve as a clue.

"Okay, the clue said we must find the source of mother's tears," Alyson said. "It seems to me the source is up there." She pointed toward the ceiling, where the water appeared to be coming from the wall.

"Oh, great." Mac moaned. "More climbing."

"I'll go up to check it out," Devon offered. "You guys stay here."

Alyson and Mac sat on the floor of the frigid room while Eli and Trevor helped Devon sort out the climbing equipment. The climb was an easy one for an experienced climber like Devon. It was only minutes until he was calling back to them that there really was an underground stream that ran along a narrow passage that seemed to ascend toward the surface. He'd check it out while the others waited for him.

"Be careful," Alyson called back as Trevor and Eli joined the girls on the floor.

Mac leaned against Eli's shoulder and Alyson rested against Trevor's. They waited in silence for several minutes before Alyson spoke. "I'm starting to get worried. It seems like Devon's been gone a long time."

"Not that long really." Trevor wrapped his arm around Alyson in comfort.

"If he doesn't get back pretty soon I'll go up to look for him," Eli volunteered, then looked down at his watch. "He's only been gone about ten minutes. We'll give him another ten, and if he's not back I'll go after him."

Tucker lay on the floor of the tunnel next to Alyson with his head in her lap. She absently scratched him behind his ears as she waited for the endless minutes to tick by.

"It's getting late," Trevor observed. "We should probably head back once Devon returns. Maybe we can pick up where we left off tomorrow."

"My stomach is telling me it's getting close to dinnertime." Mac placed her hand over her stomach, whose growl echoed off the tunnel walls.

"I have some trail mix," Alyson offered, pulling a large baggie from her pack. "And several bottles of water."

"Thanks." Mac reached her hand into the bag and took a large fistful of the homemade nut mixture.

Alyson passed the trail mix and the bottled water around to the others as they waited nervously for Devon's return.

"How much longer?" Alyson asked a few minutes later.

"About five minutes," Eli answered.

Alyson nibbled absently on a soy stick. "I hope he's okay. If any of us got hurt we'd be in a real mess. It's not like we can call 911 or something."

"I'm sure he's fine, but I can go now if you want," he said.

"No, it makes sense to wait."

A few minutes later Tucker began to thump his tail as he lifted his head from Alyson's lap and turned toward the passageway from which they had come.

"What is it, boy?" Alyson asked.

"It's just me," Devon said as he walked into the room a few seconds later.

"How'd you get around to there?" Mac asked.

"I followed the underground stream to a large room that opens up behind a waterfall. It's totally awesome. I've always wondered what a waterfall looks like from the back side and now I know."

"Wow, you're kidding." Eli stood up. "I've got to check that out."

"We all can. The left-hand tunnel at the fork we came to leads directly to the waterfall room."

Everyone stood up and followed Devon back through the right-hand tunnel to the fork in the trail and through the left-hand tunnel to the large room that opened up behind the waterfall.

"This is so cool." Eli walked to the edge of the cliff face and looked down to where the water crashed onto the rocks below.

"This must be Justice Falls." Trevor walked over to join Eli. "I think it's the only falls this large in the area."

Alyson and Mac walked up to a spot just behind Trevor and Eli and looked down.

"That's quite a drop," Alyson observed. "Maybe you guys should step back a foot or two."

Everyone continued to watch the falling water in front of them for several minutes before retreating farther back into the room to look around.

"So the million-dollar question is," Trevor began, "what does Justice Falls have to do with mother's tears and where is the next clue? We just came through the only passage leading into this room, so where do we go from here?"

Mac walked around the room, shining her flashlight on the cave's walls. "There are some hieroglyphs painted on this wall. Maybe the answer lies here."

They studied the wall paintings for several minutes, but no one could make heads or tails of them.

"Maybe we should copy some of these down to check with Booker," Mac suggested. "If anyone in the area can read ancient hieroglyphs it'd be him."

"Good idea. And maybe he can figure out what Justice Falls and mother's tears have in common," Alyson added.

"I brought a pad and a couple of pencils." Devon passed around what he had. "Let's each take a section and copy down the hieroglyphs as best we can."

The group worked in silence for a good half hour before they felt they had the gist of the story painted on the wall.

Devon looked at his watch. "We really need to head back. We'll be doing good to get back to Alyson's by seven."

They made their way back through the tunnel toward the chasm they'd once again have to cross. "Uh, guys . . . . where's our rope?" Alyson asked.

Chapter 14

"I have no idea." Devon looked down into the water below. "Maybe it came loose and fell in?"

"No way it came loose," Eli insisted. "Someone else is in here. Someone had to have taken it."

"We didn't see anyone," Trevor pointed out. "Or hear anyone. Every sound seems to echo in here. I'm sure if we had visitors we'd have heard them."

"Well, the rope didn't get up and walk away," Mac said sarcastically.

Alyson spoke up. "However the rope managed to disappear it's gone. How do we get back across?"

"We're just going to have to work our way across without the rope," Devon said.

"I so don't want to do that." Mac held on to Eli's arm. "Maybe I can just wait here. You guys can go and get a rope and bring it back."

"It's late and that would take hours," Alyson reasoned. "I'll go. Someone hold on to Tucker until I get across."

She handed the leash to Mac, then slowly started inching across the ledge. Tucker whined and pulled at the leash behind her. She feared lifting her feet so she scooted across, causing dirt and rocks to fall to the churning water below. Once she got to the other side she took a deep breath, the first one she'd taken since she started across.

"Okay, let Tucker go."

The dog scooted across with no problem.

"Okay, Dev, you and Eli are going to have to sort of sandwich Mac. One of you cross on either side. Let her hang on to you," Alyson instructed.

Devon went first, followed by Mac, and then Eli.

"Mac, open your eyes," Eli said.

"If I fall I don't want to see how high up I am."

"If you don't open your eyes you will fall," Alyson pointed out.

"Okay. But I'm going on record to say that I don't like this and I'm not having fun."

The minutes it took for the trio to get across the ledge felt like an eternity to Alyson, who was holding her breath on the other side.

"Okay. You're next, Trev," Alyson instructed as the trio arrived safely on the other side.

"Tomorrow we bring extra ropes," Mac declared as Trevor made his way to safety.

"Mom, we're back," Alyson called as the tired and dusty group walked through the door over an hour later.

"I'm in the kitchen," her mom called back. "I was starting to get worried about you. It's getting pretty late."

"I know; I'm sorry." Alyson walked over to where her mother was stirring something on the stove and gave her a hug. "We met a few more obstacles along the way than we were expecting, so everything took longer than planned."

"Did you find what you were looking for?"

"Not yet, but I feel like we're making progress. We've sort of hit a dead end at this point, though, so I was planning on calling Booker to see if he could help us figure this out."

"Why don't you fill me in over dinner? I made seafood chowder and baked bread. There's plenty to go around if you'd all like to stay."

"It smells wonderful." Mac sat down on one of the kitchen stools that lined the tile countertop. "I'll need to call my mom, though."

"I'm in." Trevor commented. "I'd like to wash up first."

"Sure," Alyson said. "You can use the bathroom near the entry hall. How about you guys?" she asked Devon and Eli.

"Sounds good." Devon sat down on one of the hardwood chairs surrounding the kitchen table. "Dad's out of town again, so Eli and I would have ended up grabbing a burger or something."

"Mac, you can use the bathroom upstairs to wash up if you want. I'm going to call Booker. I'll see if he has any insight into the whole Justice Falls situation."

Twenty minutes later everyone had made their calls, washed up, and was sitting around the table in the breakfast nook with steaming bowls of seafood chowder and slices of hot wheat bread in front of them. The chowder was thick and creamy with huge chunks of lobster, crab, shrimp, and scallops.

"What did Booker have to say?" Mac asked Alyson as she took a seat near one of the huge picture windows framing the nook.

"He wants to hear all about our adventure today and he's really interested in getting a look at those hieroglyphs. He asked if we could come by after dinner. I told him I'd check with everyone and give him a call back."

"Sure, why not?" Devon buttered a large chunk of the homemade bread. "I'd love to try to pick up tomorrow where we left off today, and any help he can give us would be great."

"I'll need to call my mom again, but since it's a Saturday night it shouldn't be a problem." Mac took a large slurp of her soup. "This chowder is excellent, Mrs. Prescott."

"Thank you, Mac. And please call me Sarah. That goes for the rest of you too. I've never been one for formality. Now tell me about your day."

They filled Sarah in on their adventure while they finished off every last bit of the chowder. There was pecan pie with vanilla ice cream for dessert, so by the time the gang piled into Devon's Expedition for the ride out to Booker's they were all full and sleepy.

"I hope Booker's got coffee." Alyson yawned as she nestled into the soft leather of the front seat. "I think the early morning combined with the late night last night is starting to catch up with me. Maybe I should have told Booker we'd meet with him tomorrow."

"Yeah, but that would put us behind," Trevor pointed out. "If we see him tonight we can continue our search tomorrow."

"Hopefully we won't come across any more gaps in the trail." Mac rested her head on Eli's shoulder. "I'm not looking forward to crossing the one we know about again tomorrow."

"You did fine on the way back," Eli said encouragingly. "You didn't slip or anything."

"I know, but I'd still rather avoid the whole thing. I don't suppose there's another way around? Like a way to access the waterfall room from above?"

Eli thought for a moment. "We might be able to use the climbing ropes to repel down the face of the cliff near the waterfall, but it'd be risky. The force of the water as it cascades is probably pretty powerful. You wouldn't want to get caught in it by accident."

"I guess I'll stick to the rope railing in the cave." Mac sat upright. "I don't think I'm ready for repelling yet."

Booker had a large pot of coffee and a warm fire waiting for them in the library. After pouring everyone a cup of the rich black liquid, he asked them to tell him everything that had happened. As they took turns revealing the details of their exploration, he stopped them many times to ask questions and have them elaborate on the details.

"I think I've dug up some information that may explain the mother's tears," Booker began as soon as they finished. "I found a local legend that there was a native tribe that lived at the foot of the cliff where the bottom of the falls is located today." Booker took a sip of his coffee. "It seems that one of the women in the tribe possessed unusual powers. I'm not sure what type of powers exactly—the legend just mentions some type of power over the elements. Anyway, the others were afraid of her, so she was ostracized by the tribe."

"How sad," Alyson sympathized.

"Just wait, it gets worse. It seems the woman had a baby who was in some way physically different. The legend speaks of the child as having the mark of evil spirits. I guess maybe he had a strange birthmark or maybe some physical deformity. Anyway, when he was just a few weeks old some of the members of the tribe stole the baby and took it to the top of the cliff, where they offered it in sacrifice to their gods."

"Oh God, they killed the baby, didn't they?" Mac groaned.

Booker nodded. "They threw if off the cliff onto the rocks below. The mother had followed them up the cliff, begging them to spare her child, and when they threw her baby off she began to cry. According to the legend, she cried nonstop for many days and nights, and her tears eventually created a mighty waterfall that flooded the valley, killing the tribe that lived there."

"That's a horrible story," Alyson said with a shiver, "but it does explain the clue. The top of the waterfall would be the source of the mother's tears."

"So now we need to figure out where to go next," Trevor added. "There wasn't a tunnel leading from that room other than the one we came in from. How do we continue on to heaven's window?"

"Let's take a look at those hieroglyphs," Booker said.

They placed their drawings on the table, trying to puzzle the pieces together in the same order as they appeared on the wall. Booker studied them silently for several minutes.

"It seems that the hieroglyphs depict some type of ceremony. My guess is that the room you found was used as a sort of temple where rituals and sacrifices were performed. I'm not sure these will help you with your puzzle, but this one picture seems to suggest that people came to the room from more than one direction. The people of the bird seemed to come from beneath the water. Was there a path running along the cliff face behind the falls?"

"I'm not sure. We didn't look around all that much," Alyson said. "There were no other entrances to the room, so if a path exists it must be outside the cave system."

"It's possible there might be a trail on the outside of the caverns that runs behind the top of the falls," Booker hypothesized. "I'd check there."

"Sounds dangerous," Mac cautioned. "Even if the trail existed during the time when these hieroglyphs were drawn, it might very well have eroded away by now."

"The parchment is only a little under two hundred years old. The trail must have been there then or why would the clues lead the traveler that way?" Eli asked.

"You could try crossing the river and looking around the cliff face on the other side. The caves may pick up there, and you might be able to climb down from the top," Booker suggested.

"Either way, I'm hearing dangerous situation," Mac reminded them.

"We can't just give up now," Trevor insisted. "We've come so far. I say we pick a strategy and check it out tomorrow. Who's with me?"

"I'm with you, but which strategy do we try?" Devon asked. "Do we go back through the tunnel and look for a way around the waterfall to another entrance, or do we repel down from the top?"

"What if the other entrance is behind the waterfall and not on the other side of the river?" Eli asked. "We'd never see it from above. I say we go back through the tunnels to see what we can find. We'll bring plenty of climbing gear. The water cascades pretty far over the lip of the cliff face. I think if we find a trail along the cliff behind it, we should be able to make it just fine."

"Makes sense to me," Devon agreed, "but anyone who isn't comfortable with the plan should feel free to bow out now."

"How about it, Mac?" Alyson asked gently. "Should we go along or let the guys handle this?"

"No, I'm in," Mac said with a groan.

Alyson squeezed her friend's hand. "It's getting late. We should all go home and get some sleep."

"I've made some progress on the journal," Booker informed them, "but since I doubt it will shed any light on the task at hand, the contents can wait for another day. Do call me when you get in tomorrow. I'll be most anxious to learn what you found."

"We will," Alyson promised. "And maybe if we get home early enough we could come by and you could share what you've discovered in the journal. If not, then Monday for sure.

"You do realize," she pointed out as they drove back up the coast from Booker's, "that even if we find a way to access the tunnel that leads to the second half of the riddle we won't be able to get any further than heaven's window until we can return at sunrise."

"That's a good point," Trevor acknowledged. "What time do you think sunrise is, anyway?"

"I think around seven twenty, give or take a few minutes," Alyson answered. "I'm usually out running with Tucker at that time, so I have a pretty good handle on sunrise."

"We could leave really early and try to make it to heaven's window by seven fifteen or so. Does anyone know how long it took us to get back from the waterfall room? It was a lot quicker than the trip in," Trevor said.

"Less than two hours," Devon answered. "But we have no idea how long it will take to get to heaven's window from mother's tears even if we do find the access point."

"I just hate to have to wait a whole week to work this out if we do manage to find heaven's window," Trevor explained.

"There's no school on Wednesday," Mac reminded them.

"Yeah, but it's the museum opening. There's no way we can miss that," Alyson said.

Trevor shrugged. "Yeah, and Thursday is Thanksgiving. So I guess that leaves Friday. I have to tell you, the suspense is killing me."

"I'd offer to leave at three o'clock in the morning, but I'm not sure how much success we'd have finding the passage behind the waterfall when it's pitch black," Mac said. "I mean, it's pitch black in the caves anyway, but it sounds like we may have to be outside for a period of time, and the idea of walking around on some narrow ledge behind that huge cascade of water scares me even in broad daylight."

"Actually," Devon pointed out, "it was totally dark in the tunnel when we crossed the chasm. It wouldn't really be that much different. I'm game for the early start if everyone else is."

"I'm in," Trevor and Eli spoke up at the same time.

"Me and my big mouth," Mac groaned in the background.

"How about you, Alyson?" Devon asked.

"Sure, why not? You can just stay over again, Mac. If we shower tonight we won't have to get up until five minutes before the guys arrive. We'll stop by your house now so you can get some clean clothes."

"Okay, then we'll meet at Alyson's at three a.m.," Devon confirmed.

Chapter 15

Sarah Prescott thought they were crazy for getting up in the middle of the night to go treasure hunting, but when Alyson pointed out that if they found the statue they could display it at the museum's grand opening, not only did she give them her blessing but she offered to make some muffins and set the coffee timer before she turned in for the night.

By the time the girls had showered and fallen into bed it was after eleven. Alyson set the alarm for a quarter till three and they fell into an exhausted slumber.

When the alarm went off both girls groaned, but they rolled out of bed, hastily donned their clothes and brushed their teeth, then stumbled down the stairs to pour themselves cups of coffee just as the guys were pulling up. As promised, there were freshly baked muffins on the counter, along with a couple of thermoses and some Styrofoam cups so they could bring additional coffee with them.

"Your mom is a goddess." Trevor wrapped his hands around a hot cup of coffee. "I have to admit, when my alarm went off even I was wondering what I was thinking, wanting to do this today."

"Well, we're up now so let's get going," Eli said, pouring his own cup of the heavenly brew.

Everyone piled into Devon's Expedition for the short drive to the cave opening. Normally they would have just walked, but this morning every minute counted. After crawling in through the cave opening they made good time to the waterfall room, arriving just a few minutes after five. Devon stopped to organize his climbing gear, then carefully made his way toward the cliff edge at the far side of the room. Securing his rope to the inside wall, he slowly edged himself around to the ledge outside the room.

"There's a path along the edge of the cliff face," he called back as he secured another clamp. "You have to swing out around the edge of the wall in order to access it, though. It looks like the part of the trail that actually connects with the room has been washed away."

"Oh, great," Mac muttered.

"I'll follow the trail to see if I can find another cave entrance," Devon told them. "No use the rest of you risking the jump if there's no entrance."

As before, the others waited nervously for Devon's return. Alyson paced, Mac curled up on the floor with Eli, and Trevor studied the wall paintings. After less than twenty minutes, Devon swung himself back into the room.

"I found the cave opening," he said. "It's just on this side of the far edge of the waterfall. The pathway along the ledge isn't too bad, but I've secured a rope handrail like we used at the chasm as an added precaution. The hardest part is going to be getting around the edge of the wall, which sort of sticks out to the ledge on the other side. You'll need to hang on and sort of swing around the corner. It's going to feel a little weird to have nothing between you and the rocks below for a few seconds, but I'll be on the other side to catch you. You won't be able to hang on to your flashlights, so you'll have to put them in your backpacks."

"What if we slip or we can't hold on to the rope?" Mac asked. "We're not all experienced climbers like you and Eli."

"Yeah, and what about Tucker?" Alyson asked.

"We can make another harness," Eli said. "I'll strap everyone in, then all you need to do is jump off the side and swing around. I'll go across with Tucker, then come back to help the rest of you."

Alyson groaned. "Tucker's going to love this." She bent down and nervously petted the puppy as Eli fashioned a harness while Devon swung back around the ledge to the other side.

Eli secured the harness around Tucker, wrapped the rope around himself, then picked up the heavy dog and walked to the edge of the cliff.

"Are you ready, Dev?" Eli called out.

"Ready."

"Okay, let's do this." Eli jumped off the ledge with the dog in his arms and swung around out of sight.

"I got them," Devon yelled back to let them know Eli and Tucker had arrived safely.

Alyson heard Tucker bark as Eli swung back around. "What's wrong? Is he okay?"

"He's fine. Devon tied him up on the other side of the waterfall," Eli informed her.

"I'll go next," Alyson offered, wanting to get to her dog as quickly as possible.

Eli ran the rope that was already attached to the wall through her legs and then around her waist. He tied it off securely, then instructed Alyson to hang on tight to the rope and try to support her weight as she swung around the ledge.

Devon was waiting to catch her on the other side. Alyson slowly made her way up to the edge of the room. She gingerly looked over the edge at the crashing water on the rocks below. The cliff room seemed higher then she remembered it, and the noise from the crashing waves was deafening. Alyson felt her legs begin to shake as she stood on the edge, preparing to fling herself out over the rocks below. She gripped the rope as tight as she could, closed her eyes, and said a quick prayer.

"It's okay," Eli yelled from beside her. "Just jump and kind of fling yourself to your left. Imagine this is a rope swing, like we had when we were kids."

I never had a rope swing as a kid, Alyson thought to herself, but she took a deep breath and swung herself around the ledge just as Eli had instructed. The journey was short but terrifying, until Devon caught her on the other side and steadied her on the ledge.

"Are you okay?" he asked as he tried to relax the death grip she had around his neck.

"Yeah, I'm okay," she said, still holding on tight.

"Grab onto the rope line I've secured along the cliff path. I need to unhook you so I can send the rope around for the next person."

Alyson did as she was told. The ledge was a good two feet wide, and with the added security of the rope that was tightly secured to the cliff face, the trek along the trail behind the waterfall didn't seem too bad.

Devon released Alyson from the makeshift harness, then swung the rope around for Eli to catch it on the other side. She heard Tucker barking from the other side of the ledge.

"I'm going across. Tucker seems frantic," Alyson told Devon.

She was cuddling the dog when Trevor joined her across the ledge a few minutes later.

The minutes ticked slowly past as they waited for Mac.

"She's really scared," Trevor whispered. "When you jumped off the ledge and dangled over the rocks for that split second, I thought she would faint."

"I was really scared too, but once I did it I realized it was kind of fun. I guess I can kind of see why Devon and Eli enjoy climbing so much. It's a real rush. I hope Mac's okay. It's been quite a while since you got here."

A few seconds later Mac came sailing around the ledge, her eyes closed tight, screaming all the way. Devon caught her and held her close while she caught her breath and regained her equilibrium. After a couple of minutes of Devon talking to her, she finally let him unhook the harness to swing it back around for Eli. Mac clung to the rope line next to Devon, her legs still shaking from the frightening experience. Eli swung around the ledge seconds later without benefit of the makeshift harness.

Finally the whole group joined Alyson, Trevor, and Tucker at the cave opening on the other side of the water.

Alyson was first in line to climb through and sink to the floor. It was totally dark in the cave, so she felt around for the flashlight that was still in her backpack. Devon and Eli wore the hardhats with lights attached and lit the way when they were on the ledge, but they would be the last to climb through. Trevor climbed through the opening just as she managed to locate her flashlight. She clicked it on so he could find his way over to her. Mac climbed through next, followed by Devon, and finally Eli.

After everyone was safely in the room they all sat down to locate flashlights and repack climbing gear.

"How are we doing on time?" Trevor asked.

"It's almost six," Devon replied. "I hope heaven's window isn't too far. I'd hate to have gotten up early and come all this way for nothing."

"Yeah, and I for one am not really up for the death swing again," Mac added. "Let's find this treasure and be done with it. If we run out of time we'll only have to come back another time."

"You do realize we'll have to swing back around the ledge on the way out," Eli reminded her.

"Oh, yeah."

They started down the dark corridor toward what they hoped was heaven's window. The tunnel was fairly wide, with good headroom. There were growths hanging from the ceiling that looked like icicles. The floor of the tunnel seemed to be fairly level, with only a slight decline in elevation.

"Were there any other clues we should be on the lookout for between mother's tears and heaven's window?" Trevor asked.

"Not that we could make out," Alyson said. "But there were a couple of lines of text we never did figure out, so who knows."

The floor of the cavern, which had been gradually descending, began to climb again. The walls narrowed somewhat but not to an uncomfortable degree. As the incline leveled off, the tunnel opened up into a large room with a large pool of water to the left and a sharp drop-off to the right. In the center of the room was a bridge between the two, which seemed to have been nature-formed rather than man-made.

"I guess we cross here," Devon said. "The bridge looks fairly sturdy. Just don't look down and you'll be fine."

"Oh, great. More acrobatics," Mac moaned.

Devon walked across first, followed by Alyson and Tucker.

"It's a piece of cake, Mac," she called back from the other side. "The bridge is as wide as the sidewalk in front of your house. Just don't look down."

"I'll walk right behind you and catch you if you stumble," Eli promised.

"Okay, here goes." Mac started slowly across the bridge, followed by Eli, then Trevor.

"See, piece of cake," Alyson said as Mac made it across.

"It might have been easier than the death swing, but I wouldn't exactly call it a piece of cake. I know you told me not to look down, but I did. It would be quite a drop if you happened to stumble a little to the right."

After everyone had made it across they hurried along the tunnel on the far side of the room, ever mindful of the minutes ticking away.

"I feel fresh air coming from up ahead," Devon called to the group behind him.

"Heaven's window," Alyson hoped.

"We figured it was a window to the outside, so that makes sense," Devon agreed.

After another couple of hundred feet the tunnel opened up into a small room with a hole in the ceiling that opened up to the sky.

"It's just starting to get light," Trevor exclaimed. "It looks like we made it in time."

"It's seven ten," Devon confirmed. "If Alyson is right in her estimate of sunrise we should only have about ten minutes to wait."

"I wonder what we're looking for," Eli said. "How will we know when the sun hits the right spot to reveal the next clue? I mean, there doesn't seem to be any way in or out of the room other than the way we came."

"I don't know," Trevor voiced the doubt everyone was feeling. "The parchment made it sound like the clue would be reveled at the moment of sunrise. I guess as soon as we see the sun come up we should start looking."

"The opening to the sky seems to be directly overhead," Mac pointed out. "Even when the sun comes up over the horizon it won't shine directly into this opening. That won't happen until midday."

"Maybe the sun reflects against something on the outside and it's the reflection that shines in through the opening," Trevor guessed.

"Hey, guys, it looks like it's getting lighter." Alyson pointed toward the opening. "Everyone, keep your eyes open for whatever happens."

At exactly seven twenty-three a bright light that looked much like a searchlight streamed through the window, illuminating a spot on the wall. The flash of light lasted only seconds, but it was enough time for them to identify the spot.

"Okay, here it is." Trevor shone his flashlight on the exact place the light had hit. "But where's the clue? I don't see anything unusual, do you?"

"The parchment said something about a cattail," Alyson remembered. "This groove in the wall sort of looks like a cattail." She wiggled her fingers inside the groove. "I think I feel something," she said just as the walls on the far side of the room groaned and moved to reveal a narrow passage.

"Wow, this is just like *Indiana Jones*," Trevor marveled as he walked across the room and squeezed through the opening. "There's a room larger than the one we were in on the other side," he called back.

After everyone had squeezed through they looked around in the darkness.

"I hope those doors don't close after a certain amount of time; we have no idea how to open them from this side," Mac said nervously.

"Hopefully we won't be in here long," Alyson comforted. "We're down to the last clue, descending into endless darkness."

It was a large room, larger than any of the others they'd been through so far. At the far side of the room was a small opening in the floor, not much bigger than a well.

"I can't see the bottom; it looks pretty deep," Alyson said.

"Hence the endless darkness," Trevor offered.

"I guess we'll have to repel down," Devon suggested.

"But we have no idea what's down there or how deep it goes," Alyson argued.

"According to the parchment, we should find the sacred room," Trevor reminded her.

"If this even is the right bottomless pit," Alyson insisted. "What if this hole leads to nowhere?"

"Everything leads somewhere." Devon began pulling his climbing supplies from his pack. "I have a two-hundred-foot rope. We'll secure the line and I'll climb down. If I get to the end of the rope before I get to the end of the hole, I'll climb back up."

Devon started down into the chasm. Eli and Trevor fed the rope into the abyss, and it disappeared as Devon climbed deeper and deeper. Suddenly the rope abruptly stopped uncoiling as a crash of thunder erupted from the darkness below.

Chapter 16

Alyson screamed.

"Hey, guys, I'm okay," Devon called up from below. "There's another tunnel, and I know this sounds strange, but I think I see a light at the end of it. Hang on; I'll check it out."

"Be careful," Alyson called down after him.

"Wow, a light at the end of the tunnel," Trevor commented. "That certainly would be a poetic place to find a treasure."

"Yeah, but it doesn't really make any sense. How can there be light all the way down there?"

"I don't know. I guess we'll find out when Devon gets back."

"Hey, guys, you've really got to come down to see this," Devon called up again a few minutes later.

"Did you find the sacred room?" Trevor called down to him.

"I think so."

"Are there piles of gold coins and jewels?" Eli asked.

"Not so much."

"How about the statue?" Alyson called. "Did you see the statue?"

"No. Just climb on down and I'll show you."

"What about Tucker?" Alyson asked.

"We'll tie a line to him and lower him down," Eli suggested.

"Poor dog. I think this whole day has been pretty traumatic for him," Mac sympathized.

After lowering Tucker down, the gang climbed down the hole one at a time.

"I have no idea how I'm going to climb back up that rope," Alyson commented as Devon caught her at the bottom.

"Wow, there really is a light at the end of the tunnel," Trevor exclaimed a few seconds later as he joined the others at the bottom.

"Come on." Devon took Alyson's hand and led her toward the light. "You've really got to see this."

The tunnel opened up into a room that was illuminated by some unknown source. It was a large room, completely covered in cave drawings. At one end a large altar was chiseled from stone, and on each side of the altar stood a mighty grizzly, also fashioned from stone, standing tall on its rear legs, as if to protect the altar from anyone who dared to disturb it. But most amazingly of all, the entire area behind the altar—the walls, the floor, and the ceiling—was covered with plants. Live plants that seemed to be growing up out of the stone.

"Wow." Alyson stood amazed. "How are these plants growing down here? And where is the light coming from? I don't see an opening to the surface anywhere. How is this possible?"

She walked over to the plants and touched one of the leaves. It was real all right. Healthy, green, and lush, and seemingly growing out of stone walls and the floor of the cavern.

"Does anyone know what kind of plants these are?" Trevor asked as he joined Alyson. "It seems impossible that they're growing down here. And there's no obvious light source, yet there's light. How is all this possible?"

Devon shrugged his shoulders. "I have no idea. I was as amazed as you are when I walked in here."

"It's called the sacred room," Alyson reminded them. "Maybe the only explanation for what we're seeing is a sacred one."

"Yeah, but still . . ." Trevor began.

"There are some things that can't be explained by science," Mac said. "And then again, maybe there's some totally logical scientific explanation for what we're seeing and we just don't know what it is."

Alyson ran her hand along the surface of the altar. It had been worn smooth with age. She imagined the room full of natives, surrounding the altar in worship and sacrifice, as a priest of some type performed an ancient ceremony. In the exact center of the altar was a slight indentation, perfectly round and smoothly polished.

"This must have been where the sacred statue sat." Alyson ran her index finger over the smooth surface. "It obviously meant a lot to the people who worshipped it. This room is amazing."

"Yeah, it really is," Trevor agreed. "I was hoping to find a room filled with gold coins and jewels, but I have to admit this room is a once-in-a-lifetime find."

"Of course we can't tell anyone about it," Alyson reminded him.

"We can't?"

"This room is obviously a sacred place. We have to be sure it remains undisturbed. I was hoping to find the statue, but now I realize it couldn't have been here. If it was, the indigenous people wouldn't have been wiped out."

"Wait a minute," Trevor interrupted. "I thought Booker said the indigenous people were killed by diseases brought here by the European settlers."

"I was a little sketchy on the whole sacred-statue-with-the-power-to-nourish-and-protect thing until I saw this room. Now I'm not so sure. Maybe the theft of the statue really was the catalyst that allowed the devastation of the native culture to occur."

"Come on, Alyson," Trevor argued. "I agree this room is amazing, and there are things contained within it that I can't explain, but do you really think the well-being of an entire culture was based on a golden statue?"

"Maybe."

"Well, one thing is for sure," Devon said, stopping the debate. "The statue isn't here now and I have no idea where to look for it."

"Yeah," Alyson acknowledged. "It would be so great to find the statue and return it to its rightful place on the altar. But like you, I have no idea where to look. It could be in some far corner of the world by now or, as Booker speculated, melted down for its monetary value. It's just so sad that someone would disturb something that obviously meant so much to an entire people."

They gathered around the altar in reverent silence. Alyson closed her eyes and imagined the chanting of the indigenous people who had once worshipped here.

"I see you found my treasure," a deep voice said from behind them.

Chapter 17

Alyson gasped and turned around to see the gardeners who had been at Booker's and in the sporting superstore. "What do you want?"

"Why, the treasure of course. Where is it?"

"We don't have it," Alyson insisted. "It's not here."

"Now why do I think you're lying?"

"I'm not," Alyson insisted. "Really. We found the room, but the treasure's gone."

"Look, there really is no treasure," Trevor added. "Alyson is telling you the truth."

"I knew there was something fishy about you," Mac accused. "How'd you find out about the treasure anyway?"

"We have a copy of the directions. Although we'd never have figured it out without you. I guess we really should thank you for that."

"You're the ones who took our rope yesterday," Mac realized. "We could have died trying to cross without it."

"You're going to die anyway. One day makes little difference."

"What do you mean, we're going to die?" Alyson demanded. Tucker growled beside her. "You're going to kill us over some treasure that doesn't even exist?"

"We've killed for less. Besides, we can't let you tell the police or anyone else about our little find."

"We won't tell. We promise," Mac blurted out. "And if we find the treasure, it's yours."

"We both know that's not likely. No, I'm afraid anyone who knows about the treasure will have to die."

Alyson thought of Booker and her mother. If the men knew about them, their lives were obviously in danger.

"Don't worry; we'll take care of your librarian friend once we have the treasure. Now where is it?"

"Look, we're telling you the truth." Devon spoke for the first time.

"All of you, get over there next to the wall. Get down on your knees."

"You think we're just going to do whatever you say?" Trevor asked. "There's only two of you and five of us."

"I think you'll do what I say if you don't want to die right now." The man pulled a gun out of his pocket and pointed it at Trevor.

Tucker started barking frantically.

"You'd better control that dog or I'll have to shoot him first."

"Tucker, quiet," Alyson commanded. She knelt down next to him and wrapped her arm around his neck. "It's okay."

Tucker continued to growl.

"What are you going to do? Shoot us?" Eli asked.

"Not yet. I might still need you to find the treasure. You seem to know how to decipher the clues. For now, I'll just leave you here until I figure out what to do next."

The men climbed up the rope, one first while the other held the gun on them, then pulled the rope up behind them.

"Now what?" Alyson started to cry. Tucker licked the tears from her face, whimpering in concern.

Devon knelt down beside her and put his arms around her. "I don't know."

"We're trapped with no way out and no one knows where we are," Mac cried. "We're going to die down here."

"Booker knows where we are," Alyson reminded her. "And my mom. They'll find us. Booker knows the clues. He'll figure it out."

"If they don't kill him first," Trevor reminded her.

"They won't kill him until they find the treasure." Alyson was certain.

"Yeah, but they might kidnap him," Mac realized. "They aren't going to let him or anyone else alert the police that we're down here."

"Like my mom?" Alyson asked. "If we don't show up in a reasonable amount of time I can guarantee you she'll alert the authorities. I'm guessing they know that. She could be in real danger."

"Okay, so we need to get out of here, and fast," Trevor concluded. "Maybe there's another way out."

Devon stood up. "Everyone spread out and look around."

They spent the next half hour searching the room for a hidden passage or entry. "This is pointless," Mac moaned. "We'll never get out of here." She sat down on the floor against the wall and rested her head on her knees.

Trevor sat down next to her and put his arm around her shoulders. "Don't give up, Mac. We've been in worst situations than this and come out on top."

"We have?" Mac asked skeptically.

"Sure; remember in the seventh grade when we were in the baseball championships and were down six to two with two outs in the ninth inning? We loaded the bases, you hit a grand slam, and we tied it up. We ended up winning in extra innings."

"That wasn't a worse situation than this." Mac smiled. "But thanks for trying to cheer me up."

"Hey, guys, look what I found," Devon said.

"A doorway?" Trevor asked hopefully.

"No, not a door but something. It looks like a latch. Like the one at heaven's door."

"Let me see." Trevor walked over and started fumbling around. "It doesn't twist open."

"Maybe you need to do something else first," Eli suggested.

"Like what?"

"I don't know. Push a lever or something. In the movies there's always a series of things that have to be done to open the secret door. Like a combination lock. You have to know what to do and what order to do it in."

"Wait. I think I know something." Alyson closed her eyes and tried to think. "Day turns to night, then back to day, one turn right will lead the way."

"Huh?" Trevor looked at her like she was crazy. "Was that on the parchment?"

"No, not the parchment. I don't know how I know it. I just heard this voice in my head."

"Alyson has received prophetic messages in her dreams before; why not while she's awake?" Mac pointed out. "Maybe we should go with it and see what we find. Can anyone think what it might mean?"

Everyone looked at Alyson.

"Hey, do I have to do everything?"

"Okay; day to night, then back to day represents a full revolution of the earth. Maybe we're looking for something shaped like the earth. Or something that represents twenty-four hours, like a clock," Trevor hypothesized.

"Or a sundial," Mac realized. "Everyone look around for something that looks like a sundial."

"Found it," Eli said from behind the altar.

"Okay, so we turn it to the right. Eli will do that while Trevor tries the latch," Mac instructed.

"Voilà," Trevor said as part of the stone wall slid open. "And look what's behind door number one."

There was a large room filled with ancient riches: gold, jewelry, pottery, furs, carvings, and weapons.

"I think we're looking at gifts and offerings to the gods for who knows how many generations," Mac guessed.

"Looks like we found our treasure." Trevor picked up a gold medallion.

"We can't take it."

"Why not, Mac? It's what we came for."

"Because it's not just a treasure. It has sacred value. Besides, it's not ours. I don't want to tempt fate by stealing from the gods. I've seen the same movies Eli has; the guy who tries to steal the gold from the sacred site always ends up dead."

"Yeah, I guess you're right."

"Is the statue there?" Alyson asked.

"I don't see it." Trevor looked around. "Sorry, but it looks like whoever wrote the message that led us here really did steal it."

"The treasure is neat and everything, but I don't see another way out. We're still trapped," Eli said.

Alyson looked around the room. The ghost from her room stood near the wall where a thick vine seemingly grew out of the wall. "Over there." She pointed. The image faded. "The way out is over there."

Devon, who was standing closest to the spot, pulled away the vine to expose a narrow opening. "By God, she's right. How'd you know?"

"Wouldn't you like to know?" she drawled.

The narrow passage led to a larger tunnel that led outside.

"Does anyone know where we are?" Alyson asked.

Trevor looked around. "Somewhere on the other side of the bluff. Near the farm where we had the Halloween party last month."

"I have cell service. I'll call my mom and have her come get us." Alyson said.

Back at Alyson's house, Sarah listened in a state of terror and fascination as Mac and the others filled her in on the events of the day while Alyson called Booker.

"And then we had to actually swing out over the rocks as the powerful waterfall crashed all around us." Mac shivered as she remembered her moment of terror.

"But wait until we tell you about the sacred room we found," Trevor interrupted. "It was totally worth the effort."

By the time Alyson returned to the warm kitchen, the story had been told and embellished, and the huge plate of sandwiches in the center of the table had been reduced to nothing but crumbs.

"Wow, thanks for saving me a sandwich," Alyson grumbled as she sat down at the oak table.

"I'll make you one," her mom volunteered. "Ham okay?"

"Yeah, thanks."

"What did Booker say?" Mac asked.

"He was totally blown away. He's going to call the cops about our visitors."

"What's he going to tell them?" Trevor asked. "If he tells them everything the secret of the cave will get out and everyone and his brother will be looking for buried treasure."

"He's going to make up a story about a break-in and abduction. I mean, technically those guys were trespassing when they were loitering on his property the other day."

"I wonder how they got a copy of the parchment," Eli said.

"They must have stolen it from Booker's house, copied it, and then put it back," Alyson surmised.

"Yeah, but how did they even know about the map?" Mac asked.

"What else did Booker say?" Devon asked.

"He was totally fascinated with the whole thing, especially the sacred room. He swears that tired old bones or not, he's going to check it out. I told him we'd be glad to take him any time he wants. It won't be hard at all now that we know about the second entrance."

"Actually, I'd like to go too." Sarah cut a huge sandwich in front of Alyson. "That is, if you go in again to take Booker."

"Sure, Mom. No problem. Maybe even next weekend if Booker's up to it. I'm sure I'll be ready to go again if I had a solid seventy-two hours of sleep."

"I hate to tell you this, Aly, but we have school tomorrow," Trevor reminded her.

"I guess we should be getting home." Mac yawned. "I'm bushed."

"I told Booker we'd come by tomorrow after school." Alyson leaned back in her chair. "He said he finished translating the journal and thinks he might be able to fill in most of the blanks about the statue."

"Oh, man," Eli complained. "Trevor and I have practice tomorrow. I hate to miss what very well may be the grand finale of this adventure."

"This little mystery of yours has totally drawn me in too," Sarah added. "How about if we invite Booker over for dinner tomorrow night so we can all hear what he has to say together?"

"Sounds fine with me," Alyson agreed. "I'll go call him back to see if he can come."

Chapter 18

School seemed to drag by at a snail's pace the next day. In an effort to kill some time before dinner, Alyson and Mac decided to catch Eli and Trevor's practice session.

"What time is it now?" Mac asked Alyson for the hundredth time.

"Three thirty-seven. Exactly nine minutes since the last time you asked me."

"I can't remember being this anxious about anything for a long time. Do you really think Booker figured out what happened to the statue?"

"He didn't exactly say he knew where it was; he just said he was able to fill in most of the missing blanks about its disappearance."

"This adventure we've been on for the past couple of months has been the most awesome experience of my life, but I really thought we'd find a treasure. Not finding the statue after all we've been through seems anticlimactic."

Alyson nervously looked at her watch again. "I know what you mean. Maybe Booker will have the missing clue that will help us figure out the statue's location. Maybe we'll find it after all." She turned back to the field. "It looks like practice is starting to wind down."

"Can't be soon enough for me," Mac commented.

After what seemed like an eternity, practice was finally over. Trevor and Eli went into the locker room to shower and change and Devon picked them all up to head to the meeting with Booker.

By the time they arrived, Alyson mother's car was already in the drive in front of the house. Booker was seated with Sarah on one of the overstuffed sofas surrounding the fireplace in the living room. A plate of finger sandwiches sat next to a large pitcher of homemade lemonade in the center of the coffee table.

"I figured we'd want to hear Booker's news first, so I made some sandwiches to tide you over until dinner," Sarah explained.

"Thanks, Mom." Alyson dropped her book bag on the floor by the door and took a seat on the sofa next to Booker.

"We've been waiting anxiously to hear what you found out." Sarah turned toward her host.

"As I told Alyson last night, I was able to finish translating the journal. It took a little ingenuity and a lot of persistence, but I think I have a fairly accurate translation. The journal, it seems, was written by the very person who stole the statue in the first place."

"You're kidding," Mac gasped. "Was it the ship's captain?"

"Let's start at the beginning. I think a full understanding of the events that led up to the removal of the statue from the altar room is necessary to really understand what happened to it and why.

"As we previously discovered," Booker began, "the *Santa Inez* docked in Cutter's Cove in 1826, but that wasn't its first journey to our shores. The ship had made several trips transporting coffee, tobacco, and other goods from exporters in the south, trading for furs and wood products in the north. Unofficially, the captain of the ship took it upon himself to participate in a quite lucrative sideline, slave trading. As we discussed in the library, warring tribes would often sell their prisoners as slaves. Any spoils of war, even human beings, were considered to be nothing more than currency."

"How awful," Sarah murmured.

"How does the statue fit in?" Trevor asked impatiently.

"I'm getting to that. It seems that one of the slaves who had been traded in 1826 was a beautiful young maiden from a neighboring tribe who had been captured during a border dispute. During her enslavement with the local tribe one of the young warriors fell in love with her. When he discovered that she had been traded to the ship's captain he made a deal with the captain to trade for her freedom."

"The statue," Alyson guessed.

"Exactly."

"But why the notes on the back of the parchment?" Mac asked. "He must have known where the sacred room was located."

"He did. But he was too superstitious to actually steal the statue from the altar room himself, so he devised a map of sorts for the captain to follow. The warrior waited on the ship in a sort of closet in his cabin while the captain went ashore to retrieve the statue. Unbeknownst to either the captain or the warrior, however, the ship's first mate had fallen in love with the same Indian girl. Somehow he had learned of the captain's plan to trade for her freedom and went after him when he left the ship."

"The captain must have told the first mate what he was doing," Mac speculated. "How else would he have known?"

"Probably," Booker agreed. "From the viewpoint of the author of the journal, he only knew that he saw the captain leave to retrieve the statue but not return. The first mate took over the captain's cabin after his demise, so the warrior knew what happened next, but he doesn't seem to know the details of what occurred."

"So the captain made a deal with the warrior to trade the statue for the native girl," Devon summarized, "unaware of the first mate's feelings for her. He shared with the first mate his plan to trade the girl for the statue. The first mate ambushed him in the gate room, either on his was in or out of the cave."

"Hence the skeleton," Alyson concluded.

"It must have happened on his way out," Mac said. "The statue is missing. Someone had to have taken it."

"The first mate could have retrieved it himself after killing the captain," Devon suggested.

"Either way, the first mate killed the captain and stole the statue," Trevor interjected. "Then what?"

"He went back to the ship and ordered the crew to prepare to set sail," Booker continued.

"Wouldn't the crew wonder about the captain?" Mac asked. "What did he tell them?"

"We don't know that," Booker admitted. "What we do know is that during the voyage the first mate took over the captain's quarters, where the warrior, who started the whole thing, was still hiding in the closet. The first mate had the slave girl brought to him in the cabin. The warrior saw an opportunity and killed the first mate in order to free his true love. He then hid both himself and the native girl in the closet until the ship landed ashore along the Baja coast. Somehow in all the confusion they managed to sneak off and eventually made their way back to this area."

"Then what?" Eli asked.

"The warrior spent most of the rest of his life looking for the statue. When he saw what was happening to his people he naturally blamed himself. He wrote the journal after his return as an accounting of his story. He believed the statue might never have made it to the ship. He was able to see what happened from his vantage point in the closet and stated that the first mate did not have it when he took over the cabin."

"We know the statue was removed from the altar room, so the first mate must either have hidden it before returning to the ship or on board somewhere but before going to the captain's cabin," Alyson guessed.

"Yeah, but why would he have hidden it off the ship if he was planning to set sail immediately?" Eli asked.

"There's no record of it being found on the ship after the cargo was confiscated," Mac reminded them.

"After the ship docked in Baja, the crew dispersed, and the cargo was confiscated, what happened to the actual ship?" Sarah asked. "Was it repaired or dismembered? Did it sink?"

No one had a good suggestion.

"If the first mate stole the statue and hid it well enough, a routine confiscation of the ship's cargo might not have revealed the whereabouts of the statue," Alyson suggested.

"That's a very good point indeed." Booker sat forward eagerly. "I'll start trying to track the eventual fate of the ship itself immediately. Maybe we can still figure out what might have happened to the statue after all. It was quite customary to simply sink badly damaged boats off shore. If the ship was sunk before the statue was found, maybe the statue is still on the boat."

"Even if we determine that the ship was sunk and we manage to find out its exact location, wouldn't the statue be ruined after spending almost two hundred years underwater?" Eli asked.

"Not at all," Booker said. "If it was made of gold and jewels as reported, it should be quite intact."

Trevor shrugged his shoulders. "The whole thing seems like a long shot to me,"

"A long shot is putting it mildly," Booker agreed. "But nothing worthwhile ever comes via the easy route. We have nothing to lose by at least trying to find out the eventual fate of the ship."

"So where do we start?" Devon asked.

"Let me do some more research to see what I can find out," Booker said. "I have quite a few contacts in the academic world. Maybe I can at least get enough information to point us in a direction."

"I'll see if I can find anything on the Web," Mac offered.

"Let's plan to get together Wednesday afternoon after the grand opening of the museum," Alyson suggested. "Maybe we'll have something by then."

"Yes," Booker agreed. "Do plan to come to my place." He turned to Sarah. "I can have Maggie make us some lunch and show you around, as promised."

"Maggie," Alyson gasped.

"Alyson, what is it?" her mom asked.

"The only other person who knew about the parchment besides the people in this room is Maggie. She has to be the one who told those treasure-robbing men about it."

"Oh, Alyson, I don't know." Booker hesitated. "Maggie's been with me for quite some time."

"Think about it. She brought in the parchment the day you found it missing. She was outside the door while we were talking. She dropped the tray she was holding and it gave her away."

"True. All right, I'll send her away until we get this sorted out. It's Thanksgiving week, and I was going to give her the weekend off anyway. I'll just start her vacation early."

"And keep everything locked up. Our gun-toting friends are still out there. Maybe you should stay with a friend or something."

"I'll tell Maggie I'm going out of town for the holiday and then check into a hotel nearby. I'll take everything I need with me and call you when I'm settled."

Chapter 19

The Cutter's Cove Market was frantic the next afternoon. Hundreds of frantic shoppers were aggressively grabbing boxes of stuffing, cans of cranberries, and bags of potatoes. Alyson and Mac had volunteered to help Alyson's mom shop for the holiday meal.

"Maybe we should have come earlier." Sarah groaned as an elderly woman ran into her with her cart as she was trying to wrestle a turkey from the fresh meat section.

"This is nuts," Alyson agreed. "Are the markets always like this two days before Thanksgiving?"

"I have no idea. Ida always did the shopping for me."

"Ida was our cook in New York," Alyson explained to Mac, who was trying to maneuver their cart toward the fresh produce aisle.

"I came with my mom last year," Mac said. "I think this is pretty much the norm."

"I thought I was going to have to break out some of my moves from my martial arts training in order to get through the crowd in front of the pumpkin pie filling," Alyson complained.

"You know martial arts?" Mac asked.

"A little. It was part of the physical education curriculum at my old school. Don't get me wrong, I'm no Bruce Lee, but I can hold my own in a fight."

"Wow, that's so cool. You'll have to show me some of your moves sometime."

"If that lady with the yellow scarf doesn't stop bogarting all the whipping cream you may get a preview right now."

"I think that about does it." Sarah rechecked her list as Alyson fought her way to the dairy case. "I'll go see if I can find a reasonably short line. You girls go by the bakery and pick up the rolls I ordered. I was going to make homemade ones, but I figured I wouldn't have time if we're going to meet with Booker tomorrow. I'll meet you at the car."

"I wonder if Booker's made any progress," Mac said as they waited in line at the bakery. "I've gotten nowhere on the Web. I actually did find information on the fate of some ships during the same time period, but nothing about the *Santa Inez*."

"Booker is pretty smart and he's traveled all over the world. He's bound to have connections."

"I hope so. Wouldn't it be cool to find the statue after all?"

"Can I help you?" the girl behind the counter asked as they finally made their way to the front of the line.

"I'm picking up rolls for Prescott."

"Here you go." The girl handed her a large bag. "Two dozen white rolls and two dozen wheat. That'll be twenty-four fifty."

Alyson handed her twenty-five dollars. "I hope Mom found a short line. The traffic seems to be getting worse." Alyson looked at her watch. "And I hope we have time to make the pies before your sisters' play. I had no idea it would take all afternoon to make a simple trip to the market."

"The play isn't until seven and it's only three thirty now. We should be okay."

Alyson's mom was just pushing the overflowing cart through the parking lot when the girls returned. After loading the back to near capacity, they made a quick trip to the florist, then headed home to make the pies.

The school cafeteria turned theater was packed when they finally arrived just before seven. Alyson looked around the room as proud parents and grandparents took snapshots of the scenery. Alyson had been part of a few piano recitals as a child but she'd never participated in a school event that garnered this much love and energy. It was awesome.

"My mom saved us seats." Mac pointed to three empty chairs near the front.

"You made it." Mac's mom moved the sweaters she had placed on the metal chairs to save them.

"Yeah, sorry we're late." Mac sat down next to her mom. "Shopping was brutal."

Alyson sat down next to Mac, with her mother next to her. "The decorations are really great," Sarah said, looking around.

"Thanks." Mac's mother leaned in closer. "I was on the decorating committee this year, as well as the costume committee. These school events are taking more time every year. More and more of the mothers have full-time jobs, so those of us who don't are left doing all the work."

"I don't have any kids in this school, but I'd be happy to help out with future events," Sarah offered.

"Sarah is an artist," Mac volunteered. "She'd be a huge help designing sets and stuff."

"Actually," Mack's mom smiled, "I'm on the committee for the carnival we have every Christmas.

I'd love to have your help. We not only have a holiday play to build sets for but we decorate the whole town. It's quite a feat."

"Sure, I'd love to help."

"There's a planning committee meeting on the Wednesday after Thanksgiving if you can make it. I'll bring the information with me when we come for dinner."

"Can I have your attention?" the narrator said from the front of the cafeteria as the lights dimmed.

The play was absolutely adorable and surprisingly well acted. Alyson couldn't remember the last time she'd experienced such a warm holiday feeling. It was fun being part of a family, even if she was living vicariously through Mac. As excited as she was to meet with Booker the next day, she found herself being even more excited for Thursday and her first noisy family holiday.

Chapter 20

Half the town turned out for the museum grand opening. After a brief presentation by the president of the historical society, Caleb cut the ribbon, which had been draped across the doorway, and the townspeople began funneling through the elaborate exhibits and media presentations.

"Can you believe this turnout?" Mac whispered to Alyson.

"I know; it's really great. Everyone has been working so hard, I'm so glad the museum is being so well received."

"The place looks really great," Trevor said from beside her. "Everyone who worked on the place should be really proud."

"Let's see if we can find Caleb to congratulate him," Devon suggested. "It's going to be hours before people clear out and we're supposed to be at Booker's at noon."

Trevor looked toward the hordes blocking the doorway. "We're never going to make our way through that."

"Don't worry," Mac said, grabbing Alyson's hand. "Alyson has ninja moves."

"She does?" Devon asked as he placed his hand on Alyson's shoulder in an attempt not to lose her.

"I think I see him over by the ancient pottery display," Eli gestured as they squeezed their way through the door.

"Yeah, I see him." Alyson changed course and headed in his direction.

"Caleb." She greeted him with a hug. "Congratulations. The place looks great. And the turnout—wow!"

Caleb hugged her back. "None of this would have been possible without you. You really should have let me thank you during the opening ceremony."

"No, this is your baby. You're the one who deserves all the credit."

"Congratulations, Caleb." Mac squeezed in from behind Alyson. "This crowd is a little overwhelming, but let's get together for a private celebration. Maybe this weekend? I know the guys want to congratulate you too, but one of the old ladies on the committee hit Devon on the shoulder with that umbrella she always carries when they tried to squeeze through."

"This weekend sounds great. Give me a call."

"Okay." Alyson kissed Caleb on the cheek. "Enjoy your fifteen minutes of fame."

They all met at Alyson's house because Booker was hiding out.

"Would it be rude to ask you to fill us in on what you've learned before we eat?" Alyson asked.

"Not at all. I've been quite anxious to share my findings. I started out by calling an associate of mine who specializes in tracking down missing or sunken ships. He's actually more of a treasure hunter than an academic, but he's the guy to talk to if you're investigating missing treasures. He informed me that the *Santa Inez* remained anchored in the same Baja harbor in which it last docked for almost a hundred years, until two rich brothers from Los Angeles bought it around the turn of the century and had it completely refurbished."

"Wow, a hundred years," Eli commented. "That's a long time to just leave a ship to rot. Didn't the ship's owners have any interest in trying to salvage it?"

"Apparently not. The cargo had already been stripped, and with the amount of damage the vessel had sustained, the company that owned it must have decided it wasn't worth saving.

"Anyway," Booker continued, "these two brothers bought the ship and turned it into a luxury liner that catered to high-end clients. I believe, from what I could find out, that the venture did very well until the Great Depression. The brothers hit hard times themselves and had to sell the ship, along with most of their other holdings, in order to make ends meet."

"So where is the ship now?" Mac asked.

"I'm not sure. I started down the path of researching that very question, but then I realized—"

"That if the ship was completely refurbished the statue would have been found then, even if it was well hidden," Sarah finished the thought.

"Exactly."

"So now what?" Trevor asked.

"I did some more checking and found that, in addition to the ship, the brothers had an extensive art collection that was auctioned off at around the same time."

"So you think they sold the statue," Mac concluded. "That is, if they ever had it. We still have no proof that the statue ever was on the ship. Is there any way we could get a list of what was sold?"

"Yes, there's a way to get a list, and yes, I've done it. The auction house that sold the collection is still in business and has records of all its past dealings. They wouldn't give me the information over the telephone, but I contacted an artist friend of mine who lives in the Los Angeles area, and he agreed to visit them to see what he could find out. Unfortunately, nothing even remotely resembling a statue was sold. It looks as if we're back to square one. I know you're disappointed, but let's not forget what we've accomplished. The discovery of the sacred room was a significant find."

"Yeah, but I really thought we'd find the statue." Mac sighed.

"We set out to find treasure and we found treasure," Trevor reminded her, "even if Alyson won't let us take any of it."

"And it has been quite an adventure," Eli added.

"The statue might not even still exist anymore," Devon concluded. "Maybe someone really did melt it down."

"Or maybe the first mate did hide it away and was killed before he could tell anyone where he stashed it," Max offered hopefully. "Maybe someday someone will find it and restore it to the altar."

"Of course without the parchment and the journal, anyone who finds it won't know what it is or where it belongs," Devon pointed out.

"The journal belongs to the museum, and Alyson could donate the parchment as well, along with a written history of the translation and the legend surrounding them, so that if anyone does find the statue at some point in the future they might be able to return it to the sacred room," Booker started. "But knowing human nature, I'd be afraid people would use the information to vandalize the sacred room and its treasure. No, I'm afraid the secret might die with us. It's a shame, really. By some twist of fate we were provided with all the pieces of the puzzle, yet we were still unable to set things right and return the statue to its rightful place."

Alyson sat quietly as they continued to debate what to do next. Should they donate the parchment to the museum? Should they bring it and the journal to the sacred room? Should they hide them away somewhere, allowing fate to once again reveal their secrets to some future explorer who might be able to complete the mission they were unable to?

"I'm afraid I really should be going," Booker announced. "I promised to stop by to visit with some old friends this afternoon. I'll let you know if I come up with any new ideas."

"I'll see you out." Alyson's mom stood up.

"We need to be going too." Devon reached over and massaged Alyson's neck to get her attention. "An old friend of my dad's is coming through town on his way up north for the holiday and we promised to be home for an early dinner with him. We'll see you tomorrow, though. I'm really looking forward to it."

"Okay," Alyson mumbled as Devon kissed her good-bye.

Alyson stared at the coffee table in front of her as Trevor and Mac also said their good-byes to Devon and Eli. The parchment had been rolled out on the table to reveal the handwritten back side, the gold medallion they had found in the cave sat beside it, and the journal rested on the table just below the medallion. Fate had brought them all the pieces to the puzzle. The odds of discovering all three and understanding their significance was astronomical. It had to be their destiny to return the statue to its rightful place.

The answer had to be somewhere on the parchment. They hadn't been able to translate the entire message. Maybe there was a vital clue they'd missed. Alyson ran the tips of her fingers gently over the rough surface, willing the parchment to speak to her through her touch.

"You know," Alyson said softly, still caressing the hastily written message, "I never did finish translating this." Her fingers stopped their wandering as she focused on the last few lines. She leaned over to take a closer look.

"Look at this. The last few lines don't really match the rest of the text. In fact, they don't look like words at all."

VO ADMNO MDBCO VAOZM
BVOZ JIZ CPIYMZY
NZQZI NOZKN OJ NVXMZY
VGOVW VWJQZ

"You're right." Mac leaned forward to see what Alyson was talking about. "In fact, a couple of the words don't even contain a vowel. I bet it's a code."

"Yeah, but why write the rest of the clue as a riddle, then write the last few lines in code?" Trevor asked.

"Maybe the beginning of the text was written by the warrior who provided the directions to the captain. He wrote them in a type of code that was familiar to him, a riddle using familiar landmarks. The captain followed the clues and found the statue. Up to this point we've been assuming the first mate surprised the captain and stole the statue after killing him, but maybe the captain had some reason to believe he was being followed and hid it, then left the directions to its location in the form of a code. A code he knew the first mate or someone else wouldn't be able to break."

"The question is, can we break that code?"

"I'm not sure. What do you think, Mac? Do you think your superior brain can figure this out?"

"Given enough time. Some codes require a specific key to work out, but others can be worked using a simple frequency chart. I suggest we try that first and see what we come up with."

"What's a frequency chart?" Trevor asked.

"If the code maker simply substituted one letter for another, say a *Q* to represent an *A*, then the frequency of the letter being used would resemble the frequency of the same letter being used in the code. In both Spanish and English, the letter *E* is the most frequently used letter, so the first step in decoding the message using this method would be to find the letter that's most frequently used in the message and substitute an *E*."

Trevor picked up a piece of scratch paper and quickly started jotting down the letters used and counting their frequency. "It looks like the most frequently used letter is a *Z*."

A-2 B-2 C-2 D-2 E-0 F-0 G-1 H-0 I-3 J-3 K-1

L-0 M-6 N-5 O-8 P-1 Q-2 R-0 S-0 T-0 U-0 V-7

W-1 X-1 Y-3 Z-9

"Okay, so let's assume that a *Z* stands for an *E*." Mac wrote out the message substituting an *E* for every Z. "The second most common letter in Spanish is an *A*, followed by an *O*. I'm assuming the code is in Spanish, not Chinook jargon. I have no idea what the most frequently used letters in that are. For now, let's use the Spanish frequency chart to try to decipher the code. The message would look like this."

V	O		A	D	M	N	O		M	D	B	C	O		V	A	O	Z	M	
o	a						a						a		o		a	e		
B	V	O	Z		J	I	Z		C	P	I	Y	M	Z	Y					
	o	a	E				e							e						
N	Z	Q	Z	I		N	O	Z	K	N		O	S		N	V	X	M	Z	Y
	e		E				a	e				a				o			e	
V	G	O	V	W		V	W	J	Q	Z										
o		a	O			o				e										

"I'm not that strong in Spanish, but it doesn't look like much," Trevor said.

"Does this method always work?" Alyson asked.

"No, not always. The shorter the passage, the less accurate the method is. Maybe we should try another language. Maybe English. The captain would probably be able to read and write English even if he was Spanish because he traded up and down the North American coast. The three most common letters in English are *E*, *T*, and *A*. Let's see what happens if we substitute those letters."

V	O		A	D	M	N	O		M	D	B	C	O		V	A	O	Z	M
a	t						t						t		a		t	e	
B	V	O	Z		J	I	Z		C	P	I	Y	M	Z	Y				
	a	t	e				e							e					
N	Z	Q	Z	I		N	O	Z	K	N		O	S		N	V	X	M	Z	Y
	e		e				t	e				t				a			e	
V	G	O	V	W		V	W	J	Q	Z									
a		t	a			a				e									

"That looks better. The first word is *at*. What's the fourth most common letter?" Alyson asked.

"*O*."

"So *M* becomes *O*?"

"Maybe. Not every letter falls in order. Once you get a few blanks filled in you use word content to figure out the rest. For example, the fifth word is a four-letter word ending in *ate*. It could be *hate*, *mate*, *late*, *gate*, or *rate*."

"Try *gate* or *mate*," Alyson suggested. "The message could be referring to the gate room or the first mate."

"Not really conclusive. The tenth word is a two-letter word starting with *T*. I'm guessing it's *to*. If it is, we can substitute *J* for *O*. If we do that, the sixth word is probably *one*. That means *I* equals *N*."

"When I look at the last word I see either *alone* or *above*. If we substitute either an *L* or *B* for *W* and either an *N* or *V* for *Q*, what does that do to the rest of the puzzle?"

Trevor scribbled a few notes on his pad. "If we assume the word is *alone*, then the eighth word is (-)

E N E N. If we assume the word is *above*, then the eighth word is (-) E V E N."

"*Seven*," Alyson guessed. "Try *above* for the last word and *seven* for the eighth word. And I bet the ninth word is *steps*. That would make *K* equal *P*. There are lots of *M*s. What's the next most frequent letter?"

"I forget. I think it's either *I* or *R*. Let's try both and see what happens."

"The *I/R* together in the second word makes me think of the word *first*. Let's substitute *D* for *I* and *R* for *M*," Alyson suggested.

V	O		A	D	M	N	O		M	D	B	C	O		V	A	O	Z	M	
a	t			i	r	s	t		r	i	g/m		t		a		t	e	r	
B	V	O	Z		J	I	Z		C	P	I	Y	M	Z	Y					
g/m	a	t	e		o	n	e				n		r	e						
N	Z	Q	Z	I		N	O	Z	K	N		O	S		N	V	X	M	Z	Y
s	e	v	e	n		s	t	e	p	s		t	o		s	a		r	e	
V	G	O	V	W		V	W	J	Q	Z										
a		t	a	r		a	b	o	v	e										

"Oh, oh, I have it," Mac shouted. "'At first right after gate one hundred seven steps to sacred altar above.'"

Trevor quickly filled in the rest of the puzzle. "By God, Mac I think you're right. The question is, what does it mean?"

"I guess it means you take the right-hand tunnel after the gate room, the one that was so tight. You walk one hundred and seven steps and there you'll find the sacred altar. I'm guessing the captain heard someone following him and hid the statue there."

"I don't remember any sacred altar down that passage," Trevor said.

"It might be a symbolic altar," Mac guessed. "We won't know for sure until we go back to check it out."

"It's pretty late today and tomorrow's Thanksgiving," Alyson reminded them. "It'll have to wait until Friday."

"Do you think the men who ambushed us before are still around?" Mac asked.

That, Alyson decided, was a very good question.

Chapter 21

Thanksgiving Day dawned sunny and unseasonably warm. Alyson could smell the turkey roasting in the oven as she made her way downstairs. She stopped, closed her eyes, and inhaled deeply. There was something about the scent of roasting turkey on Thanksgiving morning that made her feel five years old again. Of course when she was five years old it was a cook creating the heavenly scent and not her very own mother. This was so much better.

"I see you've got an early start." Alyson kissed her mom's cheek as she stood at the sink peeling potatoes.

"I've been up for hours. I made you some cinnamon rolls. They're under the warmer by the oven."

"Wow, Supermom strikes again." Alyson lifted the cover and helped herself to one of the large frosted rolls. "These look heavenly, but you really didn't need to go to all that trouble."

"I wasn't planning on making them, but I woke up before dawn and couldn't get back to sleep, so I figured why not? I certainly had the time."

"What's up with the insomnia?" Alyson asked as she poured herself a glass of milk to go with her roll. "Is something on your mind? You usually sleep like a baby."

"I guess I'm a little nervous about our dinner party today. I found my mind racing with all the stuff

I need to do and all the things I didn't want to forget to do."

"Mom, it's just my friends and their families. You've hosted dinner parties for heads of state and foreign dignitaries and never even broken a sweat."

"I know, but this is the first time I've ever thrown a dinner party on my own without the help of caters, decorators, and serving staff. I just want everything to be perfect."

Alyson sat down at the kitchen counter near where her mom was working.

"Mom, no matter how perfectly or imperfectly things turn out, I promise you, in my eyes the day will be perfect. You can burn the turkey or have lumps in the gravy and it will still be my best Thanksgiving ever. Just relax and enjoy it. Take a moment to stop and appreciate how great this really is. Just you and me on our own, sharing a special day with our friends, without maids or caterers or party planners. Besides, you're a great cook and you have me to help. Let me finish this heavenly breakfast you so lovingly made for me and I'll do whatever you want."

"You're right. In fact, I think I'll join you." Putting down the potato she was peeling, Sarah poured herself a cup of coffee and slid one of the sugary concoctions she had spent half the morning baking onto a cobalt blue plate.

"I told everyone to come over at around two," Alyson said as she helped herself to a second cinnamon roll. "I hope that's okay."

"That will be fine. The turkey will be done around then. We'll need to heat up all the other dishes while it's sitting. I figured we'd eat at around three. I bought the biggest turkey they had, but I still wasn't sure it would be enough, so I also bought a precooked ham. We can heat it in the second oven while the yams and the vegetable dishes are heating in the top oven."

"Sounds like you've thought of everything. What can I do to help?"

"Maybe you could make a centerpiece of the flowers we bought yesterday for the table, then just spread the rest around the house. Our good vases are on the top shelf of the hutch. After that maybe you could iron the tablecloth and set the table. I set the cloth I want to use on top of the ironing board in the utility room. I thought we'd use Grandma's china and silver."

"We have Grandma's china and silver? I didn't think we brought any of our personal possessions with us."

"We didn't, but your dad knew I'd really want to have them so he made arrangements to ship them to us through Donovan."

Alyson's eyes teared up. "That was so sweet. I guess I've been pretty mad at him for not coming with us when we left. I must have convinced myself that he didn't care about us at all."

"Dad loves you, Alyson. Don't ever think anything different. The sacrifice we were asking him to make was just too much. He worked so hard to create the life he had. It's not surprising he didn't want to give it up. Not only would he have had to leave his work and his friends but he knew choosing to go with us might mean he could never see his family again. It wasn't an easy choice to make."

"You did."

"And I've never regretted it for a minute. But it was still hard. Dad is very close to his siblings; I was an only child. Dad grew up in a middle-class, close-knit family with two parents who were, and still are, very much part of his life. I was mostly raised by nannies. Don't get me wrong, I love your grandmother and grandfather dearly, but I never had the kind of relationship with them that your dad has with his parents."

"I know you're right, but it still hurts that he didn't choose us. But I'm not going to let that ruin our first-ever family-and-friends-only perfect Thanksgiving Day. We have each other, we have our friends, and that's enough. More than enough." Tucker barked from the rug near the fireplace where he liked to sleep. "And we have Tucker. The best dog ever." Tucker thumped his tail on the floor several times without lifting his head. "I swear that dog understands English."

"He might at that."

Alyson threw herself into her mother-assigned chores, shuffling all her complicated dad-related emotions into a box in the back of her brain. She set the table with extra care and reverence, knowing what a miracle it was that they even had her maternal grandmother's family china and silver to use. As far as she knew, the china had been in the family for over a hundred years, and the silver had originally come to the United States from France with some long-ago relative. Her dad was very perceptive. Of all the things her mother had to leave behind when they entered the witness protection program, the silver and china probably meant the most. The only other thing her mother had of her old life was an antique ring that supposedly had been buried with her.

"The table looks great." Sarah hugged her from behind. "It looks like you may have a little of the artist in you too. The flower arrangement is spectacular."

"You think so? At first I was just going to stick a bunch of flowers in a vase, but once I started trying to arrange them into a creative bouquet the small amount of artistic potential I managed to inherit from you seemed to kick in. It was fun, and I have to say I'm really pleased with the outcome."

"Alyson, just because you've never been particularly interested in art doesn't mean you don't have innate artistic potential."

"Did you see my grade school drawings? I couldn't even pull off realistic-looking stick people." Alyson looked at the antique clock on the wall. "I'd better go up and get dressed. The gang should be here in about an hour."

Forty-five minutes later, Alyson was back downstairs wearing a new dress and adorable sandals with impossibly high heels. She stopped in the entry and looked around the tastefully decorated living room.

"So what are we missing?" Sarah asked from behind her.

"Well, we have one perfectly decorated house with just the right amount of holiday charm without being too cutesy or gaudy."

"Check."

"And one perfectly set table with a beautiful centerpiece."

"Check."

"And one heavenly smelling turkey roasting in the oven."

"Check. And let's not forget the fire burning in the fireplace, perfectly built so as not to smoke or give off too much heat, totally poetic with dancing flames and just the right amount of crackle. By the way, thanks for building it before you went up to change."

"Check. And you're welcome. So what are we forgetting?"

Sarah paused and looked around. "Football."

"Football?"

"Isn't watching football on Thanksgiving some kind of male-bonding ritual? Your dad hated football, but he always joined the guys to watch it on Thanksgiving."

"Oh, that football. Of course. I'll find it on the TV and turn it down low."

"I think we're as ready as we can be," Sarah concluded just as the doorbell rang for the first time of the day.

"And just in time." Alyson went to answer it.

"Well, Mom, I think we did it," Alyson said as she dried the china plate her mother had just hand washed. "We pulled off the perfect family-and-friends holiday. The food was fantastic and everyone seemed to get along really well and have a lot of fun."

"It was a nice day, wasn't it?"

"The best. I remember this one moment specifically. I guess you could call it a perfect moment. I had gone into the dining room to put something on the table and as I returned to the living room I just stood there for a minute and caught a glimpse of the guys as they cheered on their favorite football team. Mac's dad was yelling something about the referee needing glasses and Devon's dad was agreeing with his assessment. Devon, on the other hand, was saying something like 'no way, that was an excellent play,' and Trevor and Eli seemed to be agreeing with him. I'm not sure who Mac's brother agreed with. He was too busy stuffing your homemade artichoke dip into his mouth to really voice an opinion. After a few minutes of watching their friendly competition, I went back into the kitchen, and you were stirring the gravy while Mac's mom mashed potatoes and Mac cut up lettuce for the salad. Mac's two little sisters were sitting on the floor playing with Tucker, who was in absolute heaven. And in that moment I suddenly knew what it must be like to be from a big family complete with siblings, cousins, aunts and uncles. It was nice. Really nice."

"It was nice." Sarah handed her another plate to dry. "I'm sorry you were an only child; I guess you missed out on a lot."

"I'm not. Sorry I was an only child, that is. I can't imagine what would have happened under the current circumstances if I had siblings to take into consideration."

"I guess you're right; maybe it was for the best."

"There's one piece of pie left." Alyson held up the mostly empty pie plate. "Want to split it?"

"Sure. I'll make some coffee. I could use a break. As perfect as today was, it was certainly a lot more work than our previously catered holidays."

"The gang and I are getting together tomorrow to follow the clues contained in the code at the bottom of the parchment. If we find it, we plan to return the statue to the sacred altar. Do you want to come?"

"I'd love to. Thanks for asking. What time are you leaving?"

"Early, around seven. If the statue is where we think it is, it won't take long to find. We'll take the easier route to the sacred room, the one we found on our way out the last time."

"I wonder why the person who wrote the message didn't send the ship's captain around that way in the first place."

"I'm not sure. Maybe there were people who lived near there and he was afraid he'd be seen. Or maybe the other way wasn't all that much easier back then. The path leading across the chasm could have been intact, and the cave writings indicated that the path behind the waterfall was once quite wide."

"That's true. I'm exhausted. I think I'll go to bed. I'll see you in the morning."

Chapter 22

The next morning the gang gathered early for what they hoped would be the successful conclusion of their journey. The trip to the beginning of the first right-hand tunnel after the gate room was uneventful. Once again Devon took the lead and counted off 107 steps as the others followed.

"Do you see anything?" Trevor called from the back of the single-file line when Devon stopped walking.

"Not yet. The code said to look for the sacred altar above." Devon shone his flashlight along the narrow dirt roof overhead. "Hang on. I think I see something." Standing on tiptoe, he felt along a ridge that was several feet over his head. "I can't reach it. I'll boost you up and you see if you can feel anything," he said to Alyson, who was standing directly behind him.

Devon boosted Alyson over his head and she felt along overhead.

"I think I feel something. I need to get a little higher. Maybe a foot or so."

Eli squeezed past Mac and held on to one of Alyson's feet while Devon held the other. They lifted her up over their heads while she balanced herself while walking her hands up above her.

"I've got it. Take me down."

Devon and Eli lowered Alyson to the ground as she cradled an object wrapped in a tattered vest. Slowly she unwrapped the statue and held it up for all to see. "It's beautiful. I can't believe we really found it. It was here all the time. So close and yet…"

"I can't see," Trevor called from the back of the line in the narrow passage. "Pass it back."

Alyson passed it to Eli, who was behind her and passed it to Mac and then to Trevor. "Let's head back to show Booker and my mom," Alyson said. "I can't wait to take it back to the sacred room where it belongs."

An hour later the gang, including Booker and Sarah this time, made their way toward the altar room through the tunnel they had used to escape days before. Booker had informed Maggie that he had found the statue and that he intended to return it to the altar room the next day. As the group approached the room, they stopped and quietly peered around the corner.

"You were right," Devon whispered. "They're here."

"Yes, I guess that implicates Maggie. I rather wish it didn't." Booker sighed.

"Are you ready?" Devon whispered to the others.

"Ready."

Devon, who was armed with one of Booker's guns, skulked silently into the room. Booker, with a gun of his own, followed. Trevor and Eli went next. Alyson, Mac, and Sarah waited at the entrance, holding Tucker back but prepared to send him in if backup was needed.

"Drop your gun," Devon demanded as he snuck up behind one of the men. He dropped his gun when he felt the barrel of Devon's gun in his back.

"You too." Booker pointed his gun at the other man.

"Where'd you come from?" the man asked, dropping his gun.

"Tie them up," Devon instructed Trevor and Eli without answering.

They tied the men's hands behind their backs and their feet together loosely enough so they could walk. They led the men into the tunnel, where Alyson and the others were waiting, and led them out. Loading them roughly, they drove them to the police.

Booker told the police these were the men who had broken in and abducted him the other day. The men tried to tell the police the real story, but it seemed so far-fetched that they didn't believe them. Booker called Maggie in and confronted her with her part in the farce. She tried to deny it but finally agreed to leave the area for good in exchange for her freedom.

"It looks like all we have to do is return the statue to its rightful place," Booker said after the police had taken the men and Maggie away.

"Aren't you afraid someone will steal it?" Alyson asked. "Who knows who else Maggie might have shown the parchment to?"

"We'll return the statue and then seal the entrances," Booker said. The group agreed to meet the next morning at Alyson's house.

Chapter 23

They gathered around the altar and placed their items on its surface. Everyone had brought an item of personal value to leave as an offering, along with the statue.

"A football?" Mac asked Trevor.

"Hey, I won my first high school game with it as a freshman. It means a lot."

"Mom, your wedding ring?" Alyson asked.

"It seemed like a good time to finally move on."

"I know what you mean," Alyson said as she placed a sealed envelope that contained the photo of herself and Tiffany next to the ring.

Booker carefully set the statue into the indentation on the altar. "Well, look at that," he gasped.

"I don't believe it." Alyson grabbed Mac's arm as tears began to streak down her face.

"I know the statue's history, but I never imagined," Devon whispered.

They all joined arms and gathered around the statue, whose eyes shone with a magnificent light the moment it had been returned to its intended resting place.

Books by Kathi Daley

Come for the murder, stay for the romance.

Zoe Donovan Cozy Mystery:

Halloween Hijinks
The Trouble With Turkeys
Christmas Crazy
Cupid's Curse
Big Bunny Bump-off
Beach Blanket Barbie
Maui Madness
Derby Divas
Haunted Hamlet
Turkeys, Tuxes, and Tabbies
Christmas Cozy
Alaskan Alliance
Matrimony Meltdown
Soul Surrender – May 2015
Heavenly Honeymoon
Hopscotch Homicide – *August 2015*
Ghostly Graveyard – *October 2015*
Santa Sleuth – *December 2015*

Paradise Lake Cozy Mystery:

Pumpkins in Paradise
Snowmen in Paradise
Bikinis in Paradise
Christmas in Paradise
Puppies in Paradise
Halloween in Paradise – *September 2015*

Whales and Tails Cozy Mystery:

Romeow and Juliet
The Mad Catter
Grimm's Furry Tail
Much Ado About Felines – *July 2015*
Legend of Tabby Hollow – *September 2015*
Cat of Christmas Past – *November 2015*

Seacliff High Mystery:

The Secret
The Curse
The Relic
The Conspiracy – *October 2015*

Road to Christmas Romance:

Road to Christmas Past

Kathi Daley lives with her husband, kids, grandkids, and Bernese mountain dogs in beautiful Lake Tahoe. When she isn't writing, she likes to read (preferably at the beach or by the fire), cook (preferably something with chocolate or cheese), and garden (planting and planning, not weeding). She also enjoys spending time on the water when she's not hiking, biking, or snowshoeing the miles of desolate trails surrounding her home.

Kathi uses the mountain setting in which she lives, along with the animals (wild and domestic) that share her home, as inspiration for her cozy mysteries.

Stay up to date with her newsletter, *The Daley Weekly*. There's a link to sign up on both her Facebook page and her website, or you can access the sign-in sheet at: http://eepurl.com/NRPDf

Visit Kathi:
Facebook at Kathi Daley Books,
www.facebook.com/kathidaleybooks

Kathi Daley Teen –
www.facebook.com/kathidaleyteen

Kathi Daley Books Group Page –
https://www.facebook.com/groups/5695788231468
50/

Kathi Daley Books Birthday Club- get a book on your birthday -

https://www.facebook.com/groups/1040638412628912/

Kathi Daley Recipe Exchange -
https://www.facebook.com/groups/752806778126428/

Webpage - www.kathidaley.com

E-mail - kathidaley@kathidaley.com

Recipe Submission E-mail –
kathidaleyrecipes@kathidaley.com

Goodreads:
https://www.goodreads.com/author/show/7278377.Kathi_Daley

Twitter at Kathi Daley@kathidaley -
https://twitter.com/kathidaley

Tumblr - http://kathidaleybooks.tumblr.com/

Amazon Author Page -
http://www.amazon.com/Kathi-Daley/e/B00F3BOX4K/ref=sr_tc_2_0?qid=1418237358&sr=8-2-ent

Pinterest - http://www.pinterest.com/kathidaley/

CPSIA information can be obtained
at www.ICGtesting.com
Printed in the USA
FSHW021257261218
54696FS

9 781514 725474